力得文化
Leader Culture

Influen and Powerful

影響力字彙

洪婉婷 ◎ 著

獨創發明人物的故事 搭配字彙學習

啟動 字彙聯想記憶 學習影響力的字彙
英文字彙過目不忘 有訣竅 搭配故事學習 超有效 !!!
字彙量N倍速擴充!!!

MP3

作者序 Preface

　　剛收到這本書的邀約時，我的女兒 Sarah 剛剛出生。我跟我先生開始回想以前那不堪回首，每天硬生生的把每個單字刻在腦袋裡的日子，真是無比痛苦。當時最想要擁有的就是哆啦 A 夢的記憶吐司。相信有很多人到現在也跟我們一樣。

　　看著我家的 baby，想著要怎麼樣才可以讓我家的小女孩以後不再拿著厚厚的一疊記憶卡，啃著單字痛苦萬分但過目就忘。怎麼樣才可以利用故事書的原理，讓在吸收書本內容的同時，不知不覺的學習字彙。不僅僅知道這個字用在哪裡，怎麼用，並在字彙以外吸收一些知識。

　　感謝我的先生陳彥維與我共同創作這本書。我們搜集了古今中外不可或缺的 28 個發明物及發明家。利用說明物品及發明家的生平來介紹有用的字彙。讓『背單字』不再是枯燥無味的一件事。在這本書裡，你會學習到萊特兄弟如何發明飛機，蔡倫如何發明紙，你也會知道臉書及谷歌的由來。更棒的是，字彙就不知不覺的跑到你的腦海中。

　　這本書，送給我們可愛的女兒 Sarah，也送給想要學習 not only vocabulary but also something else 的你。

洪婉婷

編者序 Editor

　　發明指的是一個新的事物或一個新技術的出現。我們受益於許許多多的發明，它帶領我們邁向更進步的國度，我們生活也因此更便利了。而這些發明不管是古代的發明或現代的發明，發明的影響力穿透我們各個生活層面。讀著發明人物的介紹，我們感受到的不只是發明者成長的過程，更從中學習到可貴的人格特質及思考方式，這些物品也帶來變革與創新，引領我們邁向更進步的社會。

　　發明人物的感染力和影響力使得編輯部規劃了以此主題性的故事搭配字彙學習的方式，讓讀者能夠以富學習性的題材，由讀故事的方式記憶單字，回憶故事中的人物敘述，也回憶起敘述中的文句和字彙，記憶單字不再是拿本幾千單或幾萬單囫圇吞棗的死記，更不會考後就忘，所以還等什麼呢？趕快感受一下發明人物故事帶來的影響力，體驗全新的英語字彙學習，Let's Go!!!

編輯部敬上

目次 Contents

PART 1　飲食民生

PART 2　歷史懷舊

PART 3 現代實用科技

PART 4　　資訊知識

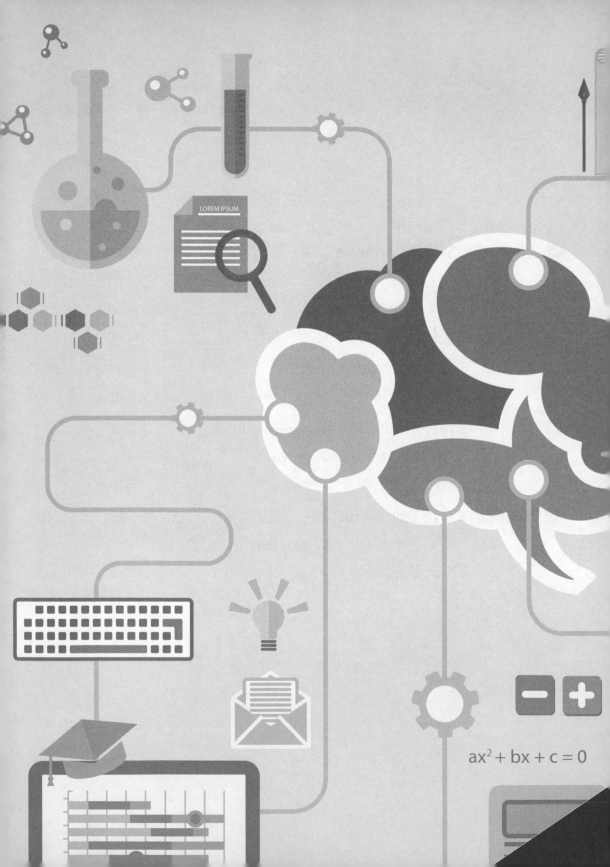

LOREM IPSUM

$ax^2 + bx + c = 0$

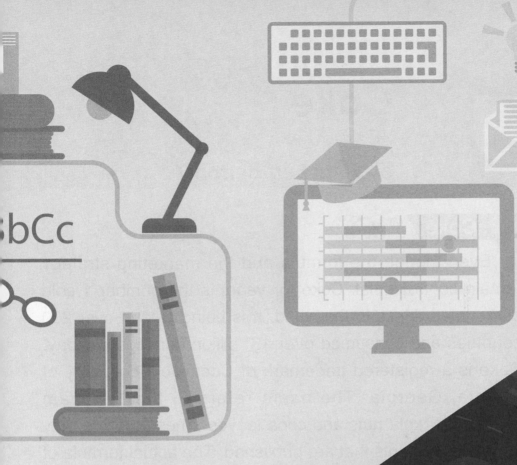

Part 1
飲食民生

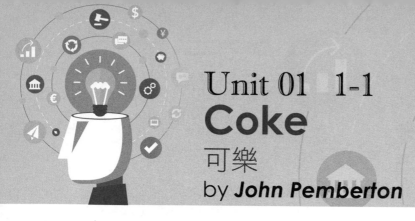

Unit 01　1-1
Coke
可樂

by *John Pemberton*

Coke MP3 01

Even though the formula and the marketing strategy remain controversial, Coke for years is the number 1 sold carbonated drinks in the world. It is being sold in over 200 countries and consumed over 1.7 billion servings per day. Coke is a registered trademark of Coca-Cola company of Atlanta, Georgia. The name refers to the two main ingredients, kola nuts and coca leaves. These are the only 2 main ingredients that are published. The actual formula of Coke remains to be a family secret. Although some companies such as Pepsi tried to recreate the drink, still no one can overcome the success of Coke.

John Pemberton, a pharmacist, invented Coke in 1886. His goal was to invent something that would bring him to commercial success. Pemberton created the syrup and combine with carbonated water which was believed that it is good for health back in the 19th century. He then claimed that Coke cured many diseases, including morphine addiction, neurasthenia and headache. Later on, Frank Robinson registered the formula with the patent office. He

01
Part
飲食民生

02
Part
歷史懷舊

03
Part
現代實用科技

04
Part
資訊知識

even designed the Coca-Cola logo and wrote the first slogan, "The Pause That Refreshes."

The actual success of Coke came in 1891 after Asa Griggs Candler bought the business. Candler decided to offer free drinks to people in order to raise the popularity. He also put the Coca-Cola logo on goods such as posters, calendars to increase the visibility. Because of his innovative marketing techniques, Coke became a national brand and became a multi billion-dollar business. It is very hard to imagine that it was once sold for only 5 cents a glass.

 可樂

　　雖然配方和營銷策略仍然存在爭議，可口可樂多年來一直是世界銷售第一的碳酸飲料。它被銷往 **200** 多個國家，每天的總銷售量超過 **170** 億份。可樂是在喬治亞州亞特蘭大市的可口可樂公司所擁有的一個註冊商標。這個名字來自兩個主要成分，可樂果和古柯葉。這兩個主成分是唯一被公布的。可樂實際的組成內容仍然是一個家族秘密。雖然有些公司如百事可樂試圖拷貝這個飲料，仍然沒有人能比可樂來得成功。

　　藥劑師約翰・彭伯頓在 **1886** 年發明了可口可樂。他的目標是創造一個能帶來商業上成功的一項產品。彭伯頓創造了藥水並結合在 **19** 世紀被認為是可以帶來健康的碳酸水。然後，他聲稱可樂能治好許多疾

病，包括嗎啡癮、神經衰弱和頭痛。後來，弗蘭克·羅賓遜在專利局為可樂成分註冊專利。他甚至還設計了可口可樂的標誌和寫了第一的口號，「The Pause The Refreshes」。

可樂的實際成功是在 1891 年阿薩·格里格斯·坎德勒收購業務之後。坎德勒決定提供免費飲料以提高能見度。他還把可口可樂標誌的放上不同商品，如海報、月曆等，以增加能見度。因為他的創新營銷技巧，可口可樂成為了國家品牌，成為一個數十億美元的生意。很難想像它曾經一杯只賣 5 美分。

必考字彙表

字彙	詞形	中譯	反義詞	中譯
Formula	n.	配方		
Strategy	n.	策略		
Controversial	adj.	爭議性的	Uncontested	無異議的
Carbonated	adj.	含二氧化碳的	Still	無氣泡的
Ingredient	n.	原料		
Publish	v.	發表	Conceal	隱蔽
Recreate	v.	再創造	Destroy	破壞
Commercial	adj.	商務上的	Nonprofit	非營利的
Combine	v.	結合	Separate	分開
Claim	v.	主張	Disclaim	否認
Addiction	n.	成癮	Detestation	嫌惡
Neurasthenia	n.	神經衰弱症	Sanity	精神健全
Slogan	n.	口號		

Visibility	*n.*	能見度	Invisibility	不可見度
Technique	*n.*	技巧	Ignorance	無知

John Pemberton MP3 02

Born on January 8th, 1831 in west central Georgia, John Pemberton is well-known for inventing Coca-Cola, A.K.A Coke. Having studied medicine and pharmacy at Reform Medical College of Georgia, Pemberton was gifted for medical chemistry. He was licensed to practice Thomsonian, which is based on botanic principles, at the age of nineteen.

Pemberton is not only a remarkable pharmacist and chemist, but also a smart businessman. He established a wholesale-retail drug business specialized in material medical. He also established laboratories, which they claimed that they are unique because all the pharmaceutical and chemical preparations used in the arts and sciences are made in house back in 1855. The most updated and improved equipment was invested in the labs as well. The original laboratory which he opened 125 years ago is still operating today, and it is now converted into the first testing labs in Georgia operating as part of the Georgia Department of Agriculture.

In April 1865 at the Civil War, Pemberton served in the Third Georgia Cavalry Battalion and was almost killed. He was wounded badly so like most veterans, he became addicted to morphine used to ease pain. As a pharmacist himself, he started working on painkillers that would serve as opium-free. This is actually the beginning of Coke invention. His business scale didn't end there. He also established his own brands of pharmaceuticals which manufactured on a large scale in Philadelphia, Pennsylvania. It is not hard to imagine his enthusiastic heart. Unfortunately, Coke did not become popular until after Pemberton passed away. He would have been so proud of his invention if he knew how successful this drink has become.

約翰・彭伯頓

　　於 1831 年 1 月 8 日出生於喬治亞西環的約翰・彭伯頓因發明可口可樂，又稱為可樂，而聞名。彭伯頓在佐治亞改革醫學院學習醫學和藥學，在醫用化學上很有天賦。他在 19 歲時便被授權實踐以植物藥學為基礎的 Thomsonian。

　　彭伯頓不僅是一個了不起的藥劑師和化學家，也是一個精明的商人。他建立了一個專攻草本的藥品批發零售企業。早在 1855 年，他還建立了實驗室。他們聲稱所使用於藝術及製藥的化學製劑都是獨一無二的。實驗室中也引進最新的設備。**125** 年前開設的原始實驗室至今仍在運轉。它現在轉換成由喬治亞州所經營的第一實驗室，為喬治亞州農業部的一部分。

在 **1865** 年 **4** 月的內戰時，彭伯頓曾在佐治亞州第三騎兵營，且差點被打死。他受傷嚴重，所以跟其他的老兵一樣，他開始沉迷於嗎啡，以緩解疼痛。作為一名藥劑師的他，開始研發無鴉片的止痛藥。這其實就是可樂發明的開頭。他的業務規模並沒有就此結束。他還在賓州的費城建立了自己品牌並量產的藥品。不難想像他的熱情的心。不幸的是，可口可樂並沒有在他有生之年成為流行。如果他知道這個飲料如此的成功，他一定會很得意自己的發明。

必考字彙表

字彙	詞性	中譯	反義詞	中譯
Well-known	*adj.*	眾所皆知的	Unknown	無人知的
Pharmacy	*n.*	配藥學		
Practice	*v.*	營業	Inaction	無活動
Wholesale	*n.*	批發	Retail	零售
Laboratory	*n.*	實驗室		
Operate	*v.*	營業	Discontinue	停止
Convert	*v.*	轉變	Keep	維持
Agriculture	*n.*	農業		
Wound	*v.*	傷害	Aid	救助
Veteran	*n.*	退役軍人	Rookie	新兵
Enthusiastic	*adj.*	熱情的	Apathetic	冷淡的

1-2　試題演練

牛刀小試

1. The company adopted his cost down _____ to increase profit.

    A. thought　　　　　B. strategy
    C. action　　　　　　D. price

2. Same sex marriage has been a _____ subject in many states.

    A. trouble　　　　　B. easy
    C. controversial　　　D. unsolvable

3. Cost and revenue are two main factors for _____ products.
    A. medical　　　　　B. non-profit
    C. daily　　　　　　D. commercial

4. "I'm loving it" is one of the best known _____ for the famous fast food restaurant.

    A. sentence　　　　　B. slogans
    C. status quo　　　　D. saying

5. About 50 to 60 years ago, the priests _____ many Taiwanese into Christianity.

   A. converted   B. communicated

   C. concluded   D. confirmed

6. Thousands of soldiers were _____ or killed in Iraq.

   A. hospital   B. blood

   C. wound   D. wounded

7. You should be _____ about your job in order to work happy.

   A. enthusiastic   B. enthuse

   C. enthusiasm   D. enthusiastically

8. Many youngsters desired to become soldiers because of the magnificent benefits _____ can get.

   A. relatives   B. soldiers

   C. parents   D. veterans

01
Part
飲食民生

02
Part
歷史懷舊

03
Part
現代實用科技

04
Part
資訊知識

1. **(B)** 此處需填入名詞，而由句意顯示 strategy 為正確解答。

2. **(C)** 此處應填入形容 same sex marriage 的形容詞，因此 A 選項可以先刪除，而由字意可以得知 controversial 為正確解答，表示同性婚姻一直是許多州具爭議性的議題。

3. **(D)** Cost and revenue 給了我們提示這裡所指的是商業用品，因此解答為 commercial。

4. **(B)** 廣告詞也是一種口號和標語，因此解答為 slogans。其中 one of the…其後名詞為複數形式，但須注意主詞為 one，故其後加單數動詞。

5. **(A)** 闡述 50~60 年前的事情因此空格需填入過去式，且其後介系詞為 into。由句意及字詞可以得到 converted 為正確解答。

6. **(D)** 此空格同 killed 需填入以過去分詞當形容詞用法的 wounded，因此 wounded 為正確解答。對等連接詞如 and, or, but 等，其後連接兩對等的詞、片語、子句、句子，故也可以其推測出考點為何，過濾掉其它選項，更精確選出合適的選項。

7. (A) 由句意可以了解空格應填入 enthuse 的形容詞，因此解答為 enthusiastic。其中 be enthusiastic about 為常見用法，表示對…感到熱忱。

8. (D) 軍人補助一般是退伍後可以獲得，因此解答應為 veterans。

Unit 02 2-1
Lego
樂高

by *Ole Kirk Christiansen*

Lego MP3 (05)

It has been 50 years since the first Lego block was made. Lego company estimated that over 400 billion Lego blocks have been produced. In another word, approximately 36 billion pieces of Lego blocks are manufactured every year. There is an amazing story behind this little brick.

Ole Kirk Christiansen, a carpenter from Denmark formed the toy company Lego in 1932. The name Lego came from the Danish phrase "leg godt" which means "play well". Lego originally was specialized in wooden toys only, but expanded to produce plastic toys in 1947. It was 1949 when Lego produced the first version of the interlocking brinks called "Automatic Binding Bricks." Two years later, plastic toys accounted for half of the Lego Company's output.

In 1954, Christiansen's son, Godtfred, became the junior managing director of Lego. He was the person who came up with the creative play idea. The Lego group then started their research and development of the brick design which is versatile and has universal locking ability. Also,

01
Part
飲食民生

02
Part
歷史懷舊

03
Part
現代實用科技

04
Part
資訊知識

they spent years finding the right material for it. Finally, on January 28th, 1958, the modern Lego brick made with ABS was patented.

Lego bricks have been popular since. Even astronauts build models with Lego bricks to see how they would react in microgravity. In 2013, the largest model was made and displayed in New York. It was a 1:1 scale model of an X-wing fighter which used over 5 million pieces of Lego bricks.

Lego might have created a lot of amazing facts, but the most incredible fact should be the universal system. Regardless of the variation in the design and the purpose of individual pieces over the years, each piece remains compatible with any existing pieces, even the one that was made in 1958.

樂高

距離第一塊被製作出的樂高積木已經有五十年。樂高公司估計，距今已生產出超過四千億塊樂高積木。換句話說，每年樂高積木的生產量約為三百六十億塊。看似簡單的一塊小磚，其實有背後個驚人的故事。

奧萊・柯克・克里斯琴森，一位來自丹麥的木匠，在 1932 年組成了樂高玩具公司。樂高這個名字來自於丹麥語的「leg godt」，就是「玩得好」的意思。樂高原本是一家專門從事木製玩具的公司，在 1947 年開始涉獵塑膠玩具，並在 1949 年創造出第一版的連扣磚，當時取名為「自動綁定磚塊」。在兩年後，塑料玩具的產量佔了樂高公司產量的一半。

1954 年，克里斯琴森的兒子，古德佛德，成為樂高的管理部初階經理。他就是想出了「創意性玩法」的人。樂高集團於是乎開始了積木的研究和開發，使得積木可具多功能性和鎖定能力。此外，他們花費了數年的時間來找到合適的材料。最後，在 1958 年 1 月 28 日，由 ABS 材質所製造的現代樂高積木取得了專利。

樂高積木從此流行。即使太空員都用樂高積木建立模型來測試他們在微重力時的反應。在 2013 年，最大的樂高模型被製作出來，並在紐約展示。這是一個 1:1 比例模型的 X 翼戰機，它使用了 500 多萬個樂高積木。

樂高可能已經創造了很多驚人的事實，但最令人難以置信的事實應該是它的通用系統。無論多年來在設計的變化或各個單片的目的，每一塊仍然與任何現有積木相容，甚至與 1958 年製造的積木也同樣相容。

必考字彙表

字彙	詞性	中譯	反義詞	中譯
Estimate	*v.*	估計	Calculate	計算

Approximately	*adj.*	大概	Exactly	確切地
Brick	*n.*	磚塊		
Form	*v.*	成立	Break	中止
Phrase	*n.*	片語		
Specialize	*v.*	專攻	Broaden	擴大
Interlock	*v.*	連結		
Bind	*v.*	綑綁	Undo	解開
Account	*v.*	佔（數量上）		
Versatile	*adj.*	多功能性	Limited	有限的
Universal	*adj.*	普遍的	Uncommon	罕見的
Astronaut	*n.*	太空人		
Microgravity	*n.*	微重力		
Variation	*n.*	變化	Similarity	類似

Ole Kirk Christiansen MP3 04

The founder of Lego, Ole Kirk Christiansen was born in a family of 12 in Jutland Denmark on April 7th, 1891. He was trained to be a carpenter, and he founded his own shop which sells daily use wooden tools such as ladders and ironing boards. However, due to the global financial crisis, the demand had fallen sharply. In order to keep the cash flow, Christiansen needed to find a new niche. He unexpectedly had an idea, and a little incident prompted him to put duck toys into production.

01
Part
飲食民生

02
Part
歷史懷舊

03
Part
現代實用科技

04
Part
資訊知識

The name of the company is derived from Danish origin, meaning playing well. Starting with a company of 7 employees, Christiansen hired all enthusiastic carpenters who had great pleasure from creating new things.

In 1942, the only facility of Lego burned down. It was then that Christiansen decided to manufacture only toys after restoration. Two years later, Christiansen officially registered the company name "LEGO".

It was 1947, when the company decided to start producing plastic toys, Ole and his son Gotdfred got the first sample of the plastic self-locking building blocks. Christiansen family then purchased the biggest injection-molding machine in Denmark and started the master production of different plastic toys. Years later, on January 28th, 1958, the Lego brick we know today was patented. In the same year, Christiansen passed away from a heart attack and Godtfred took over the business.

奧萊 • 柯克 • 克里斯琴森

樂高的創始人，奧萊 • 柯克 • 克里斯琴森在 1891 年 4 月 7 日出生於丹麥德蘭半島的一個 12 人家庭。他被培養為一位木匠，並創辦了自己的店，在店裡販售日常使用的木製工具，如梯子、燙衣板等。然而，由於全球金融危機的影響，需求大幅下滑。為了保持資金的流動，克里斯琴森需要找到一個新的利基。他意外間有了想法，而一個小事件促使他將鴨子玩具投入生產。

公司的名稱是源於丹麥文，其意思是玩得好。公司一開始只有 7 名員工，克里斯琴森聘請的木匠都富有熱誠，他們從創造新事物中得到極大的樂趣。

1942 年，樂高的唯一廠房被燒毀。就在那時，克里斯琴森決定恢復生產後只生產玩具。 2 年後，克里斯琴森正式註冊公司名稱為「樂高」。

那是 1947 年，當時該公司決定開始生產塑料玩具，奧萊和他的兒子古德佛德得到了塑料自鎖積木的第一個樣本。克里斯琴森的家庭購買了丹麥最大的注塑機，開始主生產不同的塑料玩具。幾年後，於 1958 年 1 月 28 日，我們今天所知道的樂高積木被授予了專利。同年，克里斯琴森因心臟病過世。古德佛德接手經營。

必考字彙表

字彙	詞性	中譯	反義詞	中譯
Ladder	*n.*	梯子		
Global	*adj.*	全球的	**Local**	地方性的
Crisis	*n.*	危機	**Benefit**	利益
Sharply	*adv.*	猛烈地	**Gently**	溫和地

01
Part
飲食民生

02
Part
歷史懷舊

03
Part
現代實用科技

04
Part
資訊知識

Cash flow	*ph.*	資金流動		
Niche	*n.*	利基		
Derive	*v.*	取自	Forfeit	喪失
Enthusiastic	*adj.*	熱情的	Apathetic	冷淡的
Pleasure	*n.*	愉快	Displeasure	不滿
Motto	*n.*	座右銘		
Facility	*n.*	設施		
Restoration	*n.*	重建	Abolition	消滅
Register	*n.*	登記		
Injection	*n.*	注射	Removal	去除
Mold	*v.*	鑄造		

01
Part
飲食民生

02
Part
歷史懷舊

03
Part
現代實用科技

04
Part
資訊知識

2-2 試題演練

牛刀小試

1. The engineer _____ that it would take about 2 years to come up with a new software.

   A. estimating   B. estimation

   C. estimated   D. estimate

2. Can you give me an _____ number of people that was effected by the accident?

   A. approximately   B. approximation

   C. approximated   D. approximate

3. This _____ tool can be used as a driver, a knife, and even a bottle opener.

   A. different   B. versatile

   C. multiple   D. complex

4. Superman is a _____ recognized symbol of super hero.

   A. globally   B. universe

   C. universally   D. globe

5. The _____ in water volume in Taiwan posed a major problem this summer.

A. volume   B. variation
C. value   D. valuation

6. The United States has been in economic _____ since the 911 attack.

A. boom   B. decrease
C. increase   D. crisis

7. If you are not _____ about your job, you should start to consider changing your career.

A. luxury   B. enthusiastic
C. comfort   D. prefer

8. The government has allocated funds for the _____ of the old town to attract more tourists.

A. restoration   B. abolition
C. construction   D. knock down

題目解析

1. **(C)** 名詞後應加動詞，且由後句的 would take 推測出此句為過去式，因此 estimated 為正確答案。

2. **(D)** Number 前應使用形容詞，因此解答為 approximate。指大概受到影響的人物。

3. **(B)** 語句中如 be used as a driver, a knife, and even a bottle opener 說明了這個工具具有「多功能性」，能用於這個面向，選項 a, c, d 均不符合文意，故因此答案為 versatile。

4. **(C)** Recognized 之前應加副詞，因此解答為 universally。

5. **(B)** 此句要說明的是水位的變化，因此 variation 為正確解答。

6. **(D)** 通常在形容嚴重的經濟問題，我們會慣用 crisis 這個字，因此 d 是最合適的選項。

7. **(B)** 空白處應填入形容詞，同時是在說明工作，因此 enthusiastic 為正確答案。其中 be enthusiastic about 為常見用法，表示對…感到熱忱。

8. **(A)** 由句意及字彙，我們可以簡單的選出 restoration 為最好的答案。且由其句構 for the _____ of the old town…得知應選名詞。

Unit 03 3-1
Jeans
牛仔褲
by *Jacob Davis & Levi Strauss*

Jeans MP3 05

From homeless men to multi-billionaires, no one can ever say that they have never owned a pair of blue jeans in their lives. Even Apple founder Steve Jobs wore them with a black turtleneck shirt daily as his signature look.

Jeans, originally called overalls was first designed as a practical solution to protect labors from injuries. It was during the Gold Rush-era when jeans were invented. Levi Strauss founded Levi Strauss & Co. in 1853. In 1871, his tailor Jacob Davis invented jeans, and in 1873, the two of them patented and manufactured the "XX" pants which is the famous Levis 501. It was patented under No. 139,121 for revert-reinforced pants under the heading, "Improvement in Fastening Pocket-Openings."

Originally designed for cowboys and miners, jeans became popular among young people in the 50s. It is no longer for protection but for fashion statements. Especially musicians from punk rock, heavy metal to hip hop, no one doesn't wear jeans as one of their fashion items. In the

2010s, jeans remained a popular item, and they come in different fits, including slim, cigarette bottom, boot cut, straight, etc. You name it, and they have it.

The market for jeans is amazingly big. Statistic reviews showed that in 2005, US citizens spent over 15 billion US dollars on jeans and the number keeps going up. North America accounts for 39% of global purchases for jeans, followed by Western Europe at 20%, Japan and Korea at 10% and the rest of the world at 31%. Who would have thought that a pair of pants originally designed for work nowadays became a multi billion-dollar business!

牛仔褲

從流浪漢到億萬富翁，沒有人能夠說自己從未在自己的生活裡擁有過藍色牛仔褲。即使是蘋果公司創始人史蒂夫·賈伯斯日常都以穿著牛仔褲與黑色高領衫作為自己的註冊商標。

牛仔褲，原名工作服原先是被設計當成一個實用的解決方案，以保護勞動者不受傷。牛仔褲是在淘金時代期間被發明。利維·斯特勞斯在 1853 年成立了 Levi Strauss & Co. 公司。1871 年，他的裁縫師雅各·戴維斯發明了牛仔褲。在 1873 年，他們兩個申請了「XX」褲子的專利，這也就是著名的李維斯 501。這樣產品的專利編號為 139121，內容是在「改善緊固口袋開口。」

01 Part 飲食民生

02 Part 歷史懷舊

03 Part 現代實用科技

04 Part 資訊知識

最初牛仔褲是設計給牛仔和礦工，但在 50 年代深受年輕人的喜愛。它不再只是保護，而是時尚的指標。特別是從龐克搖滾、重金屬，到嘻哈的音樂人，沒有一個人不以穿牛仔褲作為他們的時尚項目之一。在 2010 年代，牛仔褲仍然是一個受歡迎的單品，他們有不同的款式，包括超窄管、香煙腿型、喇叭褲，只要你說的出來，他們就一定有。

牛仔褲的市場是驚人的大。統計評價顯示，2005 年，美國公民花費超過一千五百億美元在牛仔褲上，且其需求數量依然不斷上升。北美佔全球牛仔褲購買率的 **39%**，其次是西歐為 **20**％，日本和韓國為 **10**％，其他國家總和為 **31**％。誰曾想到，當初為工作用所設計褲子如今盡成為了數十億美元的生意！

🔍 必考字彙表

字彙	詞形	中譯	反義詞	中譯
Homeless	*adj.*	無家可歸的		
Billionaire	*n.*	億萬富翁	Poor	貧窮的
Turtleneck	*n.*	高領毛衣		
Signature	*n.*	標誌		
Overalls	*n.*	工作褲		
Practical	*adj.*	實用的	Unrealistic	不實際的
Tailor	*n.*	裁縫師		
Revert	*v.*	恢復原狀		
Reinforce	*v.*	加強	Weaken	減弱
Fasten	*v.*	扣緊	Loosen	鬆開
Miner	*n.*	礦工		

Statement	n.	説明	Question	問題
Punk	adj.	龐克的		
Slim	adj.	纖細的	Fat	肥胖的
Statistic	adj.	統計學的		
Purchase	v.	購買	Sell	販售
Nowadays	adv.	現今	Formerly	以前

01
Part
飲食民生

02
Part
歷史懷舊

03
Part
現代實用科技

04
Part
資訊知識

Levi Strauss and Jacob Davis

Levi Strauss, born in Buttenheim, Germany on February 26, 1829 moved to the United States with his mother and two sisters when he was 18. Joining his brothers Jonas and Louis who had already begun a wholesale dry goods business in New York City, Levi decided to open his dry goods wholesale business as Levi Strauss & Co. and imported fine dry goods such as clothing, bedding, combs from his brothers in New York.

Jacob Davids on the other hand was born in Rita, today Latvia, in 1831. During his time in Riga city, he was trained and worked as a tailor. He emigrated from the Russian Empire to the United States when he was 23. He moved to San Francisco in 1856 and ran a tailor's shop there. In December 1870, Davis was asked by a customer to make a pair of strong working pants for her husband who was a woodcutter. Davis was making these working pants in duck cotton and, as early as 1871, in denim cotton. Before long, he found he could not keep up with demand.

Realizing the potential value in his reinforced jeans concept, in 1872, he approached Levi Strauss, who was still his supplier of fabric, and asked for his financial backing in the filing of a patent application. Strauss agreed, and on May 20. 1873, US Patent No. 139,121 for "Improvements in fastening pocket openings" was issued in the name of Jacob W. Davis and Levi Strauss and Company.

利維・斯特勞斯與雅各・戴維斯

利維・斯特勞斯，於 1829 年 2 月 26 日出生於德國布滕漢姆。他與他的母親，及兩個姊姊在他 18 歲時移居到美國。後來他決定加入兩個哥哥喬納斯及路易斯的乾貨批發業務，於是在舊金山開啟了利維 勞特勞斯公司，並從他紐約的哥哥那進口乾貨精品如衣服、床單、梳子等。

另一方面，雅各・戴維斯在 1831 年出生於麗塔，也就是今天的拉脫維亞。他在麗塔市的期間被訓練作為一個裁縫師。他 23 歲時從俄羅斯帝國移民到美國。他在 1856 年搬到了舊金山，並開了一間裁縫店。在 1870 年 12 月，一位客戶要戴維斯替她的丈夫做出一件堅固的工作褲給她的丈夫，因為她的丈夫是一位樵夫。早在 1871 年戴維斯便利用牛仔布做這些工作褲。不久，他發現自己已經無法跟上需求的增長。

在瞭解他的加固牛仔褲概念的潛在價值後，**1872** 年時，他找了他的布料供應商利維斯，並請求他的財務協助以申請專利。斯特勞斯同意了，並於 **1873** 年 **5** 月 **20** 日以雅各·W·戴維斯與利維·斯特勞斯公司的名義發佈美國專利號 **139121** 的「改善緊固口袋開口。」

必考字彙表

字彙	詞性	中譯	反義詞	中譯
Import	*v.*	進口	Export	出口
Fine	*adj.*	特級的	Dull	暗淡的
Bedding	*n.*	寢具		
Train	*v.*	訓練	Abandon	遺棄
Emigrate	*v.*	移民	Repatriate	遣返
Woodcutter	*n.*	伐木工人		
Duck	*n.*	帆布		
Denim	*n.*	藍粗棉布		
Demand	*n.*	需求	Supply	供應
Realize	*v.*	領悟	Misunderstand	誤解
Potential	*adj.*	潛在的		
Concept	*n.*	概念	Reality	現實
Approach	*v.*	接近	Distance	疏離
Financial	*adj.*	金融的		
Application	*n.*	申請		

3-2   試題演練

牛刀小試

1. Many Chinese _____ out from China to the United States during the 1950s.

   A. Emigrate   B. Immigrated
   C. Emigrated   D. Immigrating

2. Due to the high _____ of vegetables, the average price raised 20%.

   A. available   B. demand
   C. production   D. supply

3. While qualifying for a job, _____ experience is often more important than education.

   A. part time   B. practice
   C. practical   D. partial

4. Due to the possibility of terrorist attack, the President ordered to _____ the fort with more troops.

   A. release   B. reset
   C. reorganize   D. reinforce

5. Soon after the suicide bombing, the President of France made his first public _____.

   A. blame   B. statement
   C. thought   D. idea

6. Leonardo Da Vichi presented many new science but _____ were not understood by his generation.

   A. concepts   B. conceal
   C. concern   D. content

7. Afternoon shower announced the _____ of summer.

   A. ending   B. starting
   C. approach   D. begin

8. New York is the _____ center of the entire world.

   A. finance   B. financial
   C. financing   D. financially

01
Part
飲食民生

02
Part
歷史懷舊

03
Part
現代實用科技

04
Part
資訊知識

題目解析

1. **(C)** 此題為區分 emigrate 和 immigrate 的用法。因為是形容 1950 年代,因此應填寫過去式,又因是形容「移民出、移居國外」所以答案為 emigrated。

2. **(B)** 句尾說明菜價是上升 20%,所以空格處應填寫「需求」,解答為 demand。表示由於對蔬菜的高需求,平均價格提高了 20%。

3. **(C)** 空格應填入形容 experience 的形容詞,且句尾闡明比教育更重要,因此解答為 practical,儘管符合工作資格,實際經驗通常比教育程度更重要。

4. **(D)** 由文句及字詞即可挑選出解答為 reinforce,由於有恐怖攻擊可能性,總統下令增加更多軍隊來強化堡壘。

5. **(B)** 這裡要提及的是「公開說明」,因此解答為 statement。表示在自殺炸彈之後不久,法國總統發表第一次的公開聲明。

6. **(A)** 空格處應填入名詞,且由其後複數動詞 were 可以得知,其後需加複數名詞,而 B 選項 conceal 為動詞,故可以先刪除。而由句意可以選出 A concepts 為正確答案。

7. **(C)** 依照句意,應選擇有「開始」意味的詞彙,因此 a 可以先刪除。而依照英語習慣用語應挑選 approach。

8. **(B)** 空格處應填入形容詞，而 **D** 選項 **financially** 財政地為副詞，可以先刪除。而 **A** 和 **C** 選項分別為名詞和動名詞故均不符合。因此 **financial** 為正確解答。表示紐約是整個世界的金融中心。

01
Part
飲食民生

02
Part
歷史懷舊

03
Part
現代實用科技

04
Part
資訊知識

Unit 04 4-1
Peanut Butter
花生醬
by **Marcellus Gilmore Edson**

Peanut Butter MP3 07

Patented by Marcellus Gilmore Edson in 1884, peanut butter has been one of the most popular food in the United States for over hundreds of years. According to peanutbutterlovers.com, each American eats three pounds of peanut butter every year which in total is enough to coat the floor of Great Canyon! As popular as it is, people not only use peanut butter as bread spread, but also use it in different kinds of dishes. American children love peanut butter so much that parents even spread it on vegetables such as celeries or carrots to attract their kids to consume their daily vegetables.

Manufacturing peanut butter is rather simple. After inspection, peanut butter manufacturers roast the peanuts in special ovens. The third step is blanching, which removes the outer skin of the peanuts. Finally, the peanuts will be grounded to the desired smoothness, and add flavors such as salt by needs. Because the step of process is relatively simple, the product today is remarkably similar to that produced a century ago.

01
Part
飲食民生

02
Part
歷史懷舊

03
Part
現代實用科技

04
Part
資訊知識

Peanut butter is not only tasty but also great for your health. It contains multiple types of vitamins such as vitamin E and vitamin B6, which research shows that eating peanuts can decrease the risk of heart disease, diabetes, and other chronic health conditions. Moreover, with 180 – 210 calories per serving, peanut butter also helps you lose weight. It is because it has the enviable combination of fiber and protein that fills you up and keeps you from feeling hungry for longer. Not only tasty but also healthy, no wonder peanut butter remains one of the most popular food and keeps generating more fans over years.

花生醬

由馬塞勒斯・吉爾摩・艾德森在 1884 年獲得專利後的幾百年來，花生醬一直是美國最流行的一種食品。根據 **peanutbutterlovers.com** 的數據，每個美國人一年要購買 **3** 磅的花生醬，總數來説，足以覆蓋整個大峽谷的表面！花生醬是如此的受歡迎，以至於人們不僅用它來當麵包塗料，也將它利用在不同的菜餚。美國兒童非常喜歡花生醬，所以家長甚至把它塗在如芹菜或胡蘿蔔的蔬菜上，以吸引他們的孩子食用他們的日常蔬菜。

花生醬的製作是相當簡單的。外觀檢查結束後，花生醬廠家會用特殊烤爐烘烤花生。第三個步驟是預煮，這個步驟會除去花生的外皮。最後，花生將被研磨到期望的平滑度，並添加需要的香料，如鹽巴。由於製作過程相對簡單，今天的產品與一個世紀前的產品是非常類似的。

　　花生醬不僅味道好，也有益健康。它含有多種類型的維生素如維生素 E 和維生素 B6。研究表示，食用花生可以減少心臟疾病、糖尿病，和其他慢性健康狀況的風險。此外，每份 180 到 210 卡路里的熱量，花生醬還可以幫助你減肥。這是因為它有令人羨慕的纖維和蛋白質的組合，不但填飽你，也延長你不感到飢餓的時間。不僅味道好，而且健康，難怪花生醬仍然是最受歡迎的食品之一，愛好者年年增加 。

必考字彙表

字彙	詞形	中譯	反義詞	中譯
Popular	adj.	受歡迎的	Unpopular	不受歡迎的
Spread	n. v.	塗醬;展開	Suppress	抑制，平定
Attract	v.	吸引	Distract	使分心
Consume	v.	消耗，花費	Produce	生產
Blanch	v.	使…變白	Darken	使變黑
Remove	v.	移動，調動	Fix	使固定
Smoothness	n	平滑，流暢	Roughness	粗糙不平
Relatively	adv.	相對地	Absolutely	絕對地
Remarkably	adv.	明顯地	Usual	一般的
Tasty	adj.	可口的	Nasty	令人作噁的
Contain	v.	包含	Exclude	不包括
Decrease	v.	減少	Increase	增加
Enviable	adj.	令人羨慕的	Annoying	討人厭的
Generate	v.	產生	Destroy	破壞

Marcellus Gilmore Edson

An American inventor, George Washington Carver, born in Missouri in 1860 was known for his research in crops such as peanuts, soybeans and sweet potatoes. He invented over 100 recipes from peanuts and also developed useful products including paints, gasoline and even plastic. Because of his marvelous inventions with peanuts, he was often mistaken as the inventor of peanut butter. He might have used peanut butter in many of his recipes, but the first person to patent peanut butter in 1884 was Marcellus Gilmore Edson.

Marcellus Gilmore Edson was born on February 7th, 1849 in Montreal, Quebec, Canada. Working as a pharmacist, he often saw patients with chewing problems suffer from swallowing food. Therefore, Edson came up with the idea of peanut paste which can help people who couldn't chew well enjoy delicious food and get necessary nutrition at the same time. It might seem to be an easy thought to us now, but was a great invention back then. It was sold for six cents per pound and was very much liked by patients. He also added in sugar to change the consistency of peanut paste which became peanut candy.

Edson patented peanut butter and was issued with

01
Part
飲食民生

02
Part
歷史懷舊

03
Part
現代實用科技

04
Part
資訊知識

United States patent #306727(4) in 1884. The patent is based on the preparation of peanut paste which we call peanut butter these days. Several other people patented similar products after Edson, including John Harvey Kellogg and George Bayle. Even peanut-butter-making machine was invented by Joseph Lambert. As simple as peanut butter is, what a smart invention Edson came up with over a century ago.

馬爾賽斯‧吉爾摩‧艾德森

　　一位在 1860 年左右出生於密蘇里州的美國發明家喬治‧華盛頓‧卡爾弗因他在如花生、黃豆、番薯等作物的研究而著名 。他發明了超過 100 個花生的食譜，並利用花生開發出實用的產品，包括油漆、汽油，甚至塑膠。因為他利用花生所創造的巧妙發明，他經常被誤認為是花生醬的發明者。他也許在他的多項食譜內利用了花生醬，但第一個在 1884 年申請花生醬專利的是馬塞勒斯‧吉爾摩‧艾德森。

　　馬塞勒斯‧吉爾摩‧艾德森於 1849 年 2 月 7 日出生於加拿大，魁北克的蒙特利爾。作為一個藥劑師，他常常會看到患者由於咀嚼問題而受吞嚥食物之苦。因此，艾德森有了花生糊的想法，它可以幫助不能咀嚼的人享受美味的食物並同時獲得必要的營養。這對我們來說似乎是一個簡單的想法，但在當時卻是一個偉大的發明。它當時的售價為每磅六毛錢，並非常受到患者的青睞。他還增添了糖來改變花生糊的黏稠度，便製成了花生糖。

艾德森申請了花生醬的專利，並在 1884 年拿到美國專利＃306727（4）。該專利的內容是關於花生糊的製作基礎，也就是我們今天所稱的花生醬。繼艾德森後尚有幾位人士申請類似的產品專利，包括約翰‧哈維‧凱洛格和喬治‧培爾。約瑟夫‧藍伯特甚至發明了花生醬製造機。如此簡單的花生醬，居然是由艾德森在一個世紀多以前想出來了。

必考字彙表

字彙	詞形	中譯	反義詞	中譯
Develop	*v.*	開發	Decay	腐爛
Useful	*adj.*	有用的	Ineffectual	無效的
Include	*v.*	包含	Exclude	排除在外
Marvelous	*adj.*	令人驚嘆的	Ordinary	平凡的
Mistaken	*adj.*	誤解的	Correct	正確的
Swallow	*v.*	吞嚥	spit	吐
Delicious	*adj.*	美味的	unpalatable	難吃的
Necessary	*adj.*	必要的	needless	不需要的
Consistency	*n.*	一致性	inconsistency	前後矛盾
Preparation	*n.*	準備		
Simple	*adj.*	簡單的	Complicated	複雜的

01
Part
飲食民生

02
Part
歷史懷舊

03
Part
現代實用科技

04
Part
資訊知識

4-2　試題演練

牛刀小試

1. Her early success in her career makes her life _____ to people who have a rough life.

   A. jealous
   B. enviable
   C. envious
   D. unpopular

2. Helen Mirren always performs her parts _____. No wonder she is one of the few 2-time Golden Globe Winners.

   A. poorly
   B. tempting
   C. remarkably
   D. internationally

3. Air pollution is a serious problem. In order to solve the problem, scientists are working hard on finding the solution to _____ carbon dioxide emissions.

   A. decrease
   B. increase
   C. dismiss
   D. eliminate

4. Facebook addiction becomes a serious problem. Some people start to do crazy things in order to _____ "Like" on the social site.

   A. together   B. generate
   C. destroy   D. collection

5. Potato needs to go thru _____ process before being fried while making potato chips.

   A. chopping   B. washing
   C. darken   D. blanching

6. iPhone is a _____ invention which not only generates trillions of revenue for Apple, but also changed people's perspective for cell phones.

   A. marvelous   B. general
   C. ordinary   D. unbelievable

7. The most difficult skill for the head chief of a restaurant is to keep the quality _____ for all dishes.

   A. insurance   B. consistency
   C. equal   D. simple

8. Government now is promoting that earthquake _____ can help you save you and your families lives.

01
Part
飲食民生

02
Part
歷史懷舊

03
Part
現代實用科技

04
Part
資訊知識

A. runaway   B. produce

C. preparation   D. prepare

題目解析

1. **(B)** 此空格需填入形容詞，剛好四個選項都是形容詞，因此由句意了解應選 Unpopular（不受歡迎的）。故選 d。

2. **(C)** 此空格需填入副詞，所以 b 可以先刪除。由第二句中的 No wonder 和 Winner 可以推算，第一句的副詞應該為 remarkably。

3. **(A)** 空格在 to 之後，所以應該是填動詞。由開頭的 Air pollution 與 solve the problem 了解這是要找解決空氣污染問題的方法。因此答案為 decrease。

4. **(B)** 同上題，空格在 to 之後，所以應該要填動詞，所以 a 跟 d 可以先刪除。而由句意可以猜測 generate 就是答案。

5. **(D)** Go thru 之後應該加 ving，因此 c 可以先刪除。依照字句 before fried while making potato chips 可以推斷 blanching 為正確解答，故選 d。

6. **(A)** 此處需填入形容詞，並由句意可推測 marvelous 為正確解答表示 iPhone 是個驚為天人的發明，不僅替 Apple 創造了數兆營收，也改變了大家對手機的看法。

7. (B) 此題由 keep 會誤導需填入形容詞，但由句意和字詞可推斷應選名詞的 consistency 為正確解答。

8. (C) 此題需填入名詞，而 B 和 D 選項 produce 和 prepare 均為動詞，故可先刪除。由且由 can help you save and your families' lives 可推斷 preparation 為正確解答。

01
Part
飲食民生

02
Part
歷史懷舊

03
Part
現代實用科技

04
Part
資訊知識

Unit 05　5-1
Ketchup
番茄醬
by **Henry Heinz**

Ketchup MP3 09

Over 97% of households have a bottle of ketchup on their dinning tables in the U.S. As much as ketchup is being loved by Americans, the origins of ketchup was surprisingly not America. The name "ketchup" comes from a Chinese word which means fish sauce. In the late 17th and early 18th centuries, the British encountered ketchup, but it turned out to be a watery dark sauce which often added to soups, sauces and meats that was nothing like the ketchup today. It didn't even have the most important ingredient "tomato" in it.

The first tomato ketchup recipe was found in 1812 written by a scientist James Mease. The invention of ketchup was a huge success because the tomato growing season was short and preservation of tomato ketchups was challenging. Some producers handled or stored the product poorly that ended up with contaminated sauce. To avoid problems like this and keep the beautiful red color, some unsafe levels of preservations such as sodium benzoate were added to the commercial ketchup, which later on were proven to be harmful to health.

In 1876, Henry J. Heinz started to produce ketchup without chemicals. He developed a recipe that used ripe, red tomatoes which have more of the natural preservative. He also increased the amount of vinegar to reduce risk of spoilage. By producing the chemical free ketchup, Heinz had sold 5 million bottles of ketchup in 1905 which dominated the market.

蕃茄醬

在美國，超過 97％的家庭會在餐桌上擺上一瓶蕃茄醬。蕃茄醬被美國人所熱愛，但令人驚訝的是蕃茄醬的起源並不是美國。「Ketchup」這個名字的由來是源自於一中國字，意指魚露。在 17 世紀末和 18 世紀初，在英國發現了蕃茄醬，但它竟然是水狀的黑色醬汁，往往加入湯或醬汁或肉裡。和今天的蕃茄醬不同。它甚至沒有最重要的元素「蕃茄」在裡面。

第一個蕃茄醬的配方是在 1812 年由科學家詹姆斯・米斯所寫的。蕃茄醬的發明是個偉大的成功，因為蕃茄生長期很短，維持蕃茄醬的新鮮是具有挑戰性的。一些生產商將產品的處理或貯存不當，造成了醬汁被污染的結果。為了避免這樣的問題並保持美麗的紅色，一些商業用的蕃茄醬在裡面加入了一些過量的防腐劑，如苯甲酸鈉，這後來被證明是有害健康的。

01
Part
飲食民生

02
Part
歷史懷舊

03
Part
現代實用科技

04
Part
資訊知識

1876 年，亨利・亨氏開始生產無化學物質的蕃茄醬。他開發了一個食譜，利用成熟並更具有自然防腐效果的紅蕃茄。他也增加醋的用量，減少腐敗變質的風險。通過生產無化學製品的蕃茄醬，亨氏曾在 1905 年主導市場並銷售了 500 萬瓶蕃茄醬。

🔍 必考字彙表

字彙	詞性	中譯	反義詞	中譯
Household	*n.*	家庭	Industrial	工業的
Origin	*n.*	由來	Conclusion	結尾
Encounter	*v.*	遇見	Avoidance	逃避
Watery	*adj.*	像水的	Thick	黏稠的
Ingredient	*n.*	烹調原料		
Preservation	*n.*	防腐	Destruction	破壞
Challenging	*adj.*	具挑戰性的	Easy	簡單的
Store	*v.*	儲存	Throw away	丟棄
Contaminate	*v.*	污染	Purify	使淨化
Avoid	*v.*	避開	Face	面對
Harmful	*adj.*	具傷害性的	Harmless	不具傷害性的
Ripe	*adj.*	熟成的	Unripe	未成熟的
Vinegar	*n.*	醋		
Spoilage	*n.*	變質		

Henry J. Heinz
MP3 10

01 Part 飲食民生

02 Part 歷史懷舊

03 Part 現代實用科技

04 Part 資訊知識

Having dominated the ketchup market and brought his business to success at the age of 61, Henry Heinz was a talented businessman who was born in Pittsburgh, Pennsylvania on October 11, 1844. When Heinz was a child, he already found his way to sell vegetables and bottled horseradish at his family's garden. Even though he was young, he already knew the key to a successful business is to create differences to produce high quality products. Therefore, while he was selling prepared horseradish at his teenage years, in order to increase sales, he stood out by using clear glass containers and allowed the customers to see the quality of his products.

At the age of 25, Heinz formed his first company to sell bottled horseradish. The products were popular; however, due to the repercussions of a financial panic, the business failed. Heinz had no choice but to declare bankruptcy in 1875. A year later, he became the manager of F&J Heinz. By law, he was not allowed to start another business because of his financial problems, but in reality, Heinz was the owner of F&J Heinz. It was the same year that ketchup was added to the product line. Two years later, after his bankruptcy obligations were discharged, Heinz again changed the company name to the H.J. Heinz Company.

In 1905, Heinz became the president of the Heinz Corporation. In 1906, the Pure Food and Drug Act occurred and many food manufacturers were effected. However, because of Heinz's advocacy for its passage, his sales were increasing. Heinz passed away in 1919 and left behind a business with more than 6,500 employees and 25 factories. His products now are still being sold around the world.

亨利・亨氏

　　主導蕃茄醬市場並在他 61 歲時帶來了他企業的成功，亨利・亨氏是在 1844 年 10 月 11 日出生在賓州匹茲堡的一位天才商人。當亨氏還是個孩子時，他已經找到了自己的方式，在他家的花園裡銷售蔬菜及瓶裝辣根。儘管他很年輕，他已經知道成功的關鍵。一個成功的企業是在於創造出差異性及生產高品質的產品。因此，在他銷售辣根的少年歲月時，為了增加銷量，他利用透明的玻璃容器讓客戶看到自己產品的品質。

　　在 25 歲的時候，亨氏開了他的第一家公司，銷售桶裝辣根。該產品很受歡迎。然而，由於金融恐慌的影響，生意失敗。亨氏只好在 1875 年宣布破產。一年後，他成為了 F&J 亨氏的經理。根據法律規定，因為他的財務問題，他無法開公司，但在現實生活中，亨氏其實是 F&J 亨氏的所有者。就在同一年，番茄醬加入到該產品線。 2 年後，在他破產義務結束後，亨氏再次改變公司名稱為亨氏公司。

1905 年，亨氏成為亨氏公司的總裁。1906 年，純食品和藥品法開跑，許多食品製造商因此被影響。但是，由於亨氏公司倡導的行銷方式促使他的銷量呈逐年上升。亨氏去世於 1919 年，留下一個擁有超過 6500 名員工和 25 家工廠的企業。現在他的產品仍然被銷往世界各地。

必考字彙表

字彙	詞形	中譯	反義詞	中譯
Dominate	*v.*	統治	Follow	跟隨
Talented	*adj.*	天才的	Clumsy	笨拙的
Horseradish	*n.*	辣根		
Container	*n.*	容器		
Repercussion	*n.*	衝擊		
Declare	*v.*	申報	Conceal	隱瞞
Bankruptcy	*n.*	破產	Richness	富裕
Obligation	*n.*	法律責任		
Corporation	*n.*	股份公司		
Advocacy	*n.*	提倡	Opposition	反對
Passage	*n.*	通過	Denial	否定

5-2　試題演練

1. A mummy is a deceased human or an animal whose skin and organs have been _____.

   A. preserve   B. preservation
   C. preserving   D. preserved

2. The water was _____ by the sudden storm.

   A. pollution   B. purified
   C. contaminated   D. cleaned

3. Several _____ spectators were wounded during the terrorist attack.

   A. dangerous   B. harmless
   C. safe   D. harmful

4. The expiration date listed on each food package is to avoid people from purchasing _____ of food.

   A. contaminated   B. tasty
   C. spoilage   D. broken

5. Japanese vehicles _____ the U.S auto market since min 90s.

   A. domains   B. donates
   C. dominate   D. donuts

6. The decrease in tourism created serious _____ for the local economy.

   A. decrease   B. recession
   C. effects   D. repercussions

7. All arriving passengers are required to accomplish a Customs _____ form before entering the country.

   A. declare   B. destination
   C. declaration   D. distance

8. He was known for his _____ of human rights.

   A. avoidance   B. admission
   C. application   D. advocacy

01
Part
飲食民生

02
Part
歷史懷舊

03
Part
現代實用科技

04
Part
資訊知識

 題目解析

1. (D) 由句構 have been＋p.p 得知，空格處應填入被動式（過去分詞），因此答案為 preserved。表示木乃伊是已死去的人或動物，其皮膚跟器官一直受到保存。

2. (C) 空格處應填入被動形容詞，所以 a 可以先剔除。而由文句可以選出 contaminated 為正確解答。

3. (B) 由文句可以理解空格應填入形容詞，而 A 選項 dangerous（危險的）和 D 選項 harmful（有害的）均不符合故可以刪除，而依句意應填入「無害的」一詞，因此答案為 harmless。

4. (C) 由於空格是在 purchasing 之後，因此可能會誤以為要填入形容詞，但因為句尾為 of food，因此空格應填入名詞。正確解答為 spoilage。

5. (C) 由文句及字詞可以挑選出 dominates 為正確選項。

6. (D) 空格處應該填入名詞，因此 a 跟 c 可以先刪除，而由文句中的 economy 可選出 recession 為正確答案。表示觀光的減少對本土經濟產生了嚴重的不景氣效應。

7. (C) 這句應該常在入境時聽到，所以應該可以簡單選出答案為 declaration。

8. (D) his 為所有格其後應加入名詞，由文句可以揣測空格應填入 advocacy。表示他以倡導人權而聞名。

01
Part
飲食民生

02
Part
歷史懷舊

03
Part
現代實用科技

04
Part
資訊知識

Unit 06 6-1
Disposable Diaper
紙尿布
by *Marion Donovan*

Disposable Diaper

Diaper, one of the very first items that distinguished human from animals, was found being used from the Egyptians to the Romans. Though back then, people were using animal skins, leaf wraps, and other natural resources instead of the disposable diapers as we know today.

The cotton "diaper like" progenitor was worn by the European and the American infants by the late 1800's. The shape of the progenitor was similar to the modern diaper but was held in place with safety pins. Back then, people were not aware of bacteria and viruses. Therefore, diapers were reused after sun dry. It was not until the beginning of the 20th century, people started to use boiled water in order to reduce the common rash problem. However, due to World War II, cotton became a strategic material, so the disposable absorbent pad used as a diaper was created in Sweden in 1942.

In 1946, Marion Donovan, a typical housewife from the United States invented a waterproof covering for diapers, called the "Boater." The model of the disposable diaper was made from a shower curtain. Back then, disposable diapers were only used for special occasions such as vacations because it was considered the "luxury item." Though, the quality of the disposable diaper was not that good. The total capacity of these diapers was estimated to be around 100ml, which means it was only a one-time user.

The well known disposable diaper brand "Pampers" was created by the Procter and Gamble company in 1961. The development of the new disposable diaper was a great hit, and when the baby boom started at the 70's, the world demand exceeded the production capacity.

紙尿布

尿布,是最早區分人類與動物的項目之一。從埃及人到羅馬人都有被發現使用尿布。雖然當時人們用獸皮、樹葉和其他自然資源包裹,與我們現今所知的紙尿布有所不同。

尿布的前身在 1800 年底被歐洲及美國的嬰兒所穿著。尿布前身的形狀設計非常類似現今的尿布,但卻是使用安全別針。 那時,人們還沒有細菌和病毒的意識。因此,尿布曬乾後便再被重複使用。直到 20 世紀初,人們開始使用開水(燙尿布),這才減少了常見的皮疹問題。但由於第二次世界大戰,棉花成為了戰略物資,因此,拋棄式的尿布墊

01
Part
飲食民生

02
Part
歷史懷舊

03
Part
現代實用科技

04
Part
資訊知識

於 1942 年在瑞典被製作出來。

1946 年，瑪麗安・唐納文，一位來自美國的典型家庭主婦發明了一種防水的尿布，她稱之為「船工」。她利用浴簾製作了紙尿布的模型。當時，紙尿布由於是被認為是奢侈品，因此只有特殊場合，如休假，可以使用它。但是當時紙尿布的品質並不好。這些尿布的總容量估計約為 100ml 以下，這意味著它只能使用一輪。

眾所周知的紙尿布品牌「幫寶適」是由寶潔公司在 1961 年創造的。這個新紙尿布的發展大獲成功。開始於 70 年代的嬰兒潮使得全球的需求量超過生產能力。

必考字彙表

字彙	詞形	中譯	反義詞	中譯
Distinguish	*v.*	區別	Connect	連結
Resource	*n.*	資源		
Disposable	*adj.*	拋棄式的	Reusable	可重複使用的
Progenitor	*n.*	始祖	Descendant	後裔
Reduce	*v.*	減少	Increase	增加
Strategic	*adj.*	戰略的	Unplanned	未計畫的
Absorbent	*adj.*	能吸收的	Impermeable	不透水的
Typical	*adj.*	典型的	Unusual	不尋常的
Waterproof	*adj.*	防水的	Permeable	有滲透性的
Occasion	*n.*	場合		
Luxury	*n.*	奢侈品	Misery	窮困

| Capacity | *n.* | 容積 | | |
| Estimate | *v.* | 估計 | | |

01
Part
飲食民生

02
Part
歷史懷舊

03
Part
現代實用科技

04
Part
資訊知識

Marion Donovan   MP3 12

Marion Donovan, born in a family where her father and brother are both inventors, it would be hard for her not to have the inventive spirit. During World War II, as a housewife and a mother of two, Donovan used her creative mind on many things to help herself with her busy life. In order to ease her job from repetitively changing her children's cloth diapers, bed sheets and clothing, she came up with the idea of the diaper cover. She used the shower curtain and successfully created a waterproof diaper cover. She also added the snap fasteners to replace the safety pins to reduce the possibility of careless injuries.

Even though her invention was brilliant, no manufacturers bought the idea. Donovan had no choice but to start the production herself. The product debuted at Saks Fifth Avenue in 1849. She also applied a patent for it and received the patent in 1951.

She then started her invention of a fully disposable diaper. She had to recreate a type of paper that was not only strong and absorbent, but also conveyed water away from the baby's skin. Her creation was a great success but no one saw the demand back then. People thought it was superfluous and impractical. It was not until 1961 when Pampers was created did the disposable diaper become a hit item.

Throughout her extraordinary life, Donovan explored numerous ventures besides diapers. She had a total of 20 patents and also received an Architecture degree from Yale University in 1958.

瑪麗安・唐納文

　　瑪麗安・唐納文，出生在一個爸爸與哥哥都是發明家的家庭中，她很難不具備創新的精神。在第二次世界大戰期間，作為一個家庭主婦和兩個孩子的母親，唐納文在很多事情上利用她的創意思維，以幫助自己忙碌的生活。為了緩解重複更換孩子們的布尿布、床單和衣服的工作，她有了尿布罩的想法。她利用浴簾，成功打造了防水尿布罩。她還添加了按扣來取代安全別針，以減少許多不小心受傷的可能性。

　　儘管她的發明是聰穎的，沒有廠家同意她的想法。唐納文只好開始自己生產。她的產品於 1849 年首次在薩克斯第五大道（百貨公司）亮相。她同時申請了專利，並在 1951 年獲得專利。

爾後，她開始了紙尿布發明。她必須重新創造一個類型的紙張不僅強韌，吸水性強，而且還能使水遠離寶寶的皮膚的紙。她的創作是一個偉大的成功，但當時沒有人看見需求。人們認為這是多餘的，不切實際的。直到 1961 年，幫寶適的創建成為了紙尿布一炮走紅的原因。

在她不平凡的一生中，唐納文探索尿布以外的眾多冒險。她一共擁有 20 項專利，並於 1958 年獲得了耶魯大學的建築學學位。

字彙

字彙	詞性	中譯	反義詞	中譯
Inventive	*adj.*	發明的	Uncreative	缺乏創造性的
Repetitively	*adv.*	重複地	Infrequently	不常的
Snap fastener	*ph.*	按扣		
Recreate	*v.*	再創造		
Convey	*v.*	傳達	Receive	接收
Superfluous	*adj.*	不必要的	Basic	基本的
Impractical	*adj.*	不切實際的	Practical	實際的
Extraordinary	*adj.*	非凡的	Average	一般的
Numerous	*adj.*	眾多的	Few	稀少的
Venture	*n.*	冒險	Surety	保證

6-2　試題演練

牛刀小試

1. Education is important because children normally cannot _____ between the truth and a lie.

   A. distance　　　　　B. understand
   C. distinguish　　　 D. develop

2. Nuclear power plants produce a lot of dangerous waste which need to be_____ of and creates environmental problems.

   A. dispose　　　　　B. disposable
   C. disposing　　　　D. disposed

3. Yogurt contains helpful _____ which is good for our stomach.

   A. worm　　　　　　B. germ
   C. bacteria　　　　　D. food

4. The evolutional towel is as _____ as a sponge, yet as thin as a piece of paper.

   A. absorb   B. absorbable
   C. absorbful   D. absorbent

5. Paris Hilton was raised in a life of _____ and wealth.

   A. money   B. liberal
   C. free   D. luxury

6. People with OCD often need to do certain things _____, otherwise, they feel insecure.

   A. 10 times   B. separately
   C. repetitively   D. over and over

7. In the culture of Japan, a bow at a forty-five degree angle _____ deep respect.

   A. meaning   B. show
   C. translates   D. conveys

8. Josh was recognized for his _____ progress in math this past year.

   A. extraordinary   B. improvement
   C. extra   D. improve

01
Part
飲食民生

02
Part
歷史懷舊

03
Part
現代實用科技

04
Part
資訊知識

題目解析

1. (C) 由句中的 between 我們可以簡單選出 distinguish 為正確答案。表示教育是重要的，因為小孩通常無法分辨真相和謊言。Distinguish 為常考用法，常見的有 distinguish between A and B 還有 distinguish A from B。

2. (D) Dangerous waste 是需要「被」丟棄的，表示核能發電廠製造了許多需要處理且產生環境問題的廢棄物，因此正確解答為 disposed，表示處理的常見片語有 be disposed of 和 deal with。

3. (C) 由句意及詞彙我們可以簡單得知 bacteria 為正確答案。表示優格含有有益菌對我們胃很好。

4. (D) as ＿＿＿＿＿ as 應該填入形容詞或副詞，A 選項 absorb 為動詞故不考慮，分別考量其餘三選項(B) absorbable (C) absorbful (D) absorbent，因此 absorbent 為正確解答。

5. (D) B 選項 liberal 與 C 選項 free 均為形容詞故不考慮，由句意可以簡單得知解答為 luxury。

6. (C) 空白處應填入副詞，而由句意及字彙 repetitively 為正確解答。

7. (D) 由句意我們知道應填入「表示」一詞，因此 **conveys** 為正確答案。且依語法主詞為 **a bow** 故須選單數動詞，故 **A** 選項 **meaning** 和 **B** 選項 **show** 均不考慮，表示日本文化中，45 度鞠躬表示深深的尊敬。

8. (A) 空白處應填寫形容 **progress** 的形容詞，因此答案為 **extraordinary**。表示約翰因為他去年數學非凡的進步而受到認可。

Unit 07 7-1
Light bulb
燈泡
by *Thomas Edison?*

Light bulb MP3 13

If you think that Thomas Edison invented first light bulb, you are technically wrong. There were several people invented light bulb, but Thomas Edison mostly got credited for it because he was the person who created the first practical light bulb that is available for the general public.

76 years before Thomas Edison filed the pattern application for "Improvement in Electric Lights", Humphrey Davy invented an electric battery. When he connected wires to the battery and a piece of carbon, the carbon glowed. That was the first electric light ever invented. Though, it was not ready for the general use because the light didn't last long enough, and it was too bright for practical use. Years after, several other inventors tried to create light bulbs but no practical products were created. It was even made with platinum which the cost of platinum made it impractical for commercial use.

During the next 50 years, many inventors did different prototype of light bulbs but could not produce enough lifetime to be considered an effective product. Until 1874, Canadian inventors Henry Woodward and Mathew Evans built different sizes and shapes of carbon rods held between electrodes in glass cylinders filled with nitrogen. It was the basic design of a light bulb.

Interestingly, Thomas Edison started his research into developing a practical incandescent lamp at the same period of time. In 1879, he bought the pattern from Woodward and Evans and continued to improve upon his original design. Edison and his team discovered that a carbonized bamboo filament would last over 1200 hours. In 1880, Edison's company Edison Electric Light Company manufactured light bulbs commercially.

燈泡

如果你認為愛迪生發明第一個燈泡，嚴格上來說你是錯誤的。世上有幾個人發明了電燈泡，但湯瑪斯・愛迪生得到大部分的榮耀，因為他創造了第一個可用於一般大眾的實用電燈泡。

早在湯瑪斯・愛迪生提出「電燈的改善」專利的 76 年之前，漢弗萊・戴維發明了電池。當他連接了導線、電池與一塊碳，碳發光了。這是首個電燈的發明。不過，由於無法長時間維持光亮，且光線太亮，所以這個發明還沒準備好被實際應用。幾年後，其他幾個發明家也試圖創造燈泡，但沒有實用的產品被創作出來。有人甚至提出用鉑作為材料，但鉑金的成本無法作為商業用途。

在接下來的 50 年中，許多發明人進行了不同原型的燈泡，但還是無法創造出足夠壽命的有效產品。直到 1874 年，加拿大發明家亨利‧伍德沃德和馬修‧埃文斯以不同尺寸及形狀的電極放在碳棒之間並放入充入氮氣的玻璃瓶中。這完成了一個燈泡的基本設計。

有趣的是，湯瑪斯‧愛迪生也在相同的時間開始自己研發實用的白熾燈。愛迪生在 1878 年申請了第一個專利申請「電燈的改善」。在 1879 年，他買了伍德沃德和埃文斯的專利，並不斷改善他的原始設計。愛迪生和他的研究小組發現，碳化竹絲可以持續壽命超過 1200 小時。 1880 年，愛迪生的公司：愛迪生電燈公司開始生產商用燈泡。

必考字彙表

字彙	詞性	中譯	反義詞	中譯
Practical	*adj.*	實用的	Unrealistic	不切實際的
General	*adj.*	大眾的	Unique	特殊的
Improvement	*n.*	改進	Deterioration	退化
Connect	*v.*	連結	Disconnect	使分開
Platinum	*n.*	白金		
Commercial	*adj.*	商業的	Non-profit	非營利的
Prototype	*.n.*	樣品	Copy	副本
Lifetime	*n.*	壽命		

Consider	v.	考慮	Ignore	忽略
Effective	*adj.*	有效的	Ineffective	不有效的
Electrode	*n.*	電極		
Cylinder	*n.*	鋼瓶		
Nitrogen	*n.*	氮氣		
Incandescent	*adj.*	白熱的	Dull	昏暗的
Filament	*n.*	燈絲		

Thomas Edison MP3 14

The man that acquired a record number of 1,093 patents, Thomas Edison is mostly known for the invention of light blub.

He was mostly home schooled. During his home school years, he was working part time on the railroad between Detroit and Port Huron, Michigan, where his family then lived. But because of his passion in science, he once almost blew up the entire train car; therefore, he got fired.

Edison was working as a telegrapher and traveled around the country during the Civil War. Edison had developed hearing problems later on, so he began to invent devices that would help make things possible despite his deafness. In 1869, he quit telegraph and started to pursue invention full time.

In 1878, Edison focused on inventing a safe, inexpensive electric light. He set up the Edison Electric Light Company and began research and development. In 1880, the company found out that carbonized bamboo can be a viable alternative for the filament, which proved to be the key to a long-lasting light bulb. In 1881, the light bulb became available to the public. Edison also created the world's first industrial research laboratory known as the "Wizard of Menlo Park," in New Jersey. He had become one of the most famous men in the world by the time he was in his 30s.

湯瑪斯・愛迪生

擁有 1093 項專利的人，湯馬斯・愛迪生大多是因燈泡的發明而聞名。

愛迪生主要是在家裡接受教育。在他的家校歲月裡，他在密西根州的底特律和休倫港間的鐵路兼職，這時他的家人正住在那裡。因為他對科學的熱情，他有一次差點炸毀了整個車廂。他因此被解僱。

愛迪生在內戰期間是一位電報員，他旅行於全國各地。愛迪生有了聽力問題以後，他便開始發明可以幫助即使是耳聾的他也可工作的設備。1869 年，他放棄了電報，並開始全職於他的發明事業。

1878 年，愛迪生專注於發明一種安全，廉價的電燈。他成立了愛迪生電燈公司，並開始研究和開發。1880 年，該公司發現了炭化竹可以為長絲，這是讓長效燈泡變可能的一個關鍵。1881 年，燈泡開始提供給大眾。愛迪生也創造了世界上第一個被稱為新澤西「精靈門洛帕克」的工業研究實驗室。他在 30 歲時已經成為世界上最有名的人。

 字彙

字彙	詞形	中譯	反義詞	中譯
Acquire	*v.*	取得	Forfeit	喪失
School	*v.*	教育	Misguide	引入歧途
Passion	*n.*	熱情	Indifference	冷淡
Entire	*adj.*	全部的	Partial	部分的
Telegrapher	*n.*	電報員		
Develop	*v.*	發展出	decline	衰退
Deafness	*n.*	聾		
Pursue	*v.*	從事	quit	放棄
Carbonize	*v.*	碳化		
Viable	*v.*	可行的	Unfeasible	不可行的
Alternative	*adj.*	替代的	Conventional	普通的
Industrial	*adj.*	工業的	Domestic	家庭的

01 Part 飲食民生

02 Part 歷史懷舊

03 Part 現代實用科技

04 Part 資訊知識

7-2　試題演練

牛刀小試

1. Qualifications are important but _____ experience is always an advantage.

   A. actual　　　　　B. yearly
   C. daily　　　　　 D. practical

2. It is always excited to see the _____ before the new car release.

   A. test drive　　　B. sample
   C. prototype　　　D. copy

3. This medicine is famous for it's extremely _____ cure for a headache.

   A. effectiveness　　B. efficient
   C. effect　　　　　D. effective

4. It is very common these days for one bank to _____ another bank.

   A. combine　　　　B. sale
   C. acquire　　　　D. purchase

5. Parents should understand their kids' _____ and help them pursue their dreams.

   A. problem
   B. encouragement
   C. passion
   D. request

6. Over time, their acquaintance _____ into a lasting friendship.

   A. became
   B. changed
   C. transformed
   D. developed

7. Most people spend years _____ fortune and never realize money isn't happiness.

   A. pursuing
   B. gaining
   C. become
   D. chased

8. I am afraid your plan is not economically _____.

   A. variable
   B. visible
   C. valuable
   D. viable

01
Part
飲食民生

02
Part
歷史懷舊

03
Part
現代實用科技

04
Part
資訊知識

 **題目解析**

1. (D) 此空格應填入形容 experience 的形容詞,因此 practical 為正確解答。

2. (C) 此處應填入用來形容汽車的樣品,因此我們會選擇 prototype 而不是 sample。

3. (D) 此處應填入形容 cure 的形容詞,因此 effective 為正確解答。表示藥品是以治療頭痛特別有效而聞名。

4. (C) 由句意可以理解應選有「併購」意味的動詞,to 之後要加原形動詞,而 B 選項 sale 為名詞故可以先刪除,在比較其餘 3 選項,A 選項的意思是結合不合句意,D 選項的意思為購買故選擇 C 因此解答為 acquire。

5. (C) 由句意可理解空格處應填入形容小孩的熱情,依句構來看,因此解答為 passion。

6. (D) 由句意可以理解空格處應填入形容友情的轉變,又因後面加了 into,因此 developed 為正確答案,故選 d。

7. (A) 此空格應填入有追求意味的動詞,spend 後加 ving 為慣用法,因此選 A pursuing 表示許多人花了數年追求財富,卻未曾了解到金錢不等同快樂。

8. (D) 此句構為 I'm afraid＋that 子句，子句中句構為 S＋v＋not＋adv＋_____，空格只能填形容詞，而由句意及字詞可知 viable 為正確答案。

01
Part
飲食民生

02
Part
歷史懷舊

03
Part
現代實用科技

04
Part
資訊知識

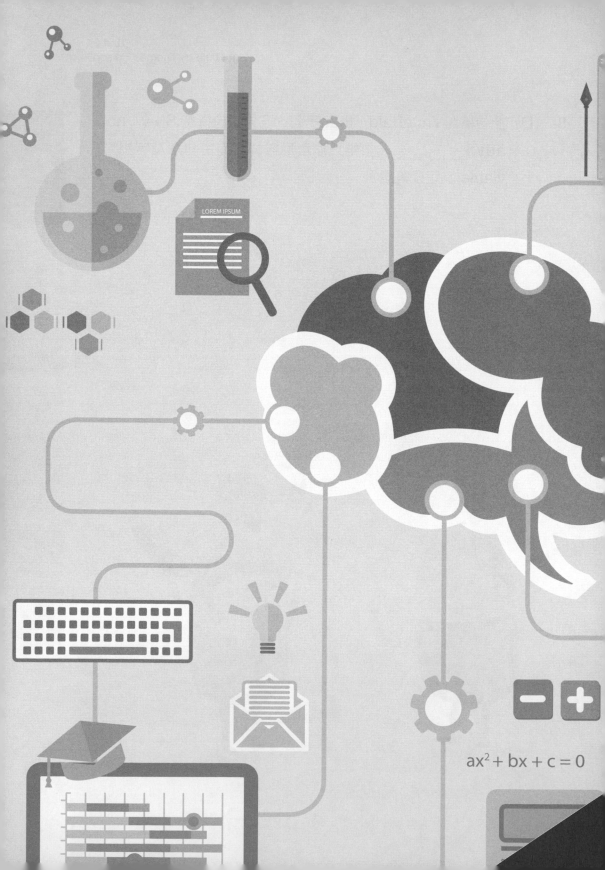

Part 2
歷史懷舊

Unit 08 8-1
Steam Engine
蒸汽引擎

by *Thomas Newcomen*

Steam Engine
MP3 15

The scene where Jack and Rose were chased by the police in the hot steamy engine room must be unforgettable for the Titanic movie fans. Titanic, a 52,310-ton boat which planned to travel from Southampton to New York actually was powered by 24 double-ended and 5 single-ended boilers feeding reciprocating steam engines. As you can imagine how a powerful steam machine could be.

A steam engine is a heat engine that performs mechanical work using steam as its working fluid. People have been using the steam machine to create power for hundreds of years. It could be as small as an iron to as powerful as the Titanic.

The first steam machine was patented by a Spanish inventor in 1606. After that, several steam machine related patents were filed but none of them were practical. Thomas Savery, in 1698, patented first practical, atmospheric pressure steam engine of one horse power, though it was not very effective and could not work beyond a limited depth

Unit 08
Steam Engine by Thomas Newcomen

01
Part
飲食民生

02
Part
歷史懷舊

03
Part
現代實用科技

04
Part
資訊知識

of around thirty feet.

It was not until 1712, when Thomas Newcomen invented the first commercial steam engine using a piston for pumping in a mine. Steam engine started to be widely used in various products. James Watt patented a steam engine that produced continuous rotary motion in 1781. Another 100 years later by 1883, steam engines were already able to be applied to vehicles and trains. Steam engines was one of the moving forces behind the Industrial Revolution.

蒸汽機

電影鐵達尼號的粉絲一定很難忘傑克和蘿絲在炎熱潮濕的機房被警察追逐的畫面。鐵達尼號，一艘 52310 噸重，計畫由南安普敦前往紐約的船，實際上搭載了 24 個雙鍋爐和 5 個單鍋爐往復式蒸汽機。你可想而知蒸汽機有多麼強大的力量。

蒸汽機是一個利用蒸氣啟動動能來執行工作的熱動能機器。幾百年來，人們不停使用蒸氣機來創造動力。它可以小到一個蒸氣熨斗，大到如巨大的鐵達尼號。

第一台蒸汽機的專利在 1606 年由一位西班牙發明家所提出。爾後，陸續有幾個相關的專利提出，但卻不實用。1698 年，湯瑪士・薩弗里提了第一個實用且具有一匹馬力的氣壓蒸汽機。雖然效用不大，無法在超出約三萬英尺的深度下工作。

直到 1712 年，湯馬仕‧紐科利用活塞的方式發明了第一個用在礦井的商業蒸汽機。 蒸汽機開始被廣泛用於各種不同的產品。詹姆斯‧瓦特，在 1781 年申請了連續旋轉運動的蒸汽機專利。再過 100 年後的 1883 年，蒸汽機已經能夠應用於汽車和火車。蒸汽機是工業革命背後的動力之一。

必考字彙表

字彙	詞形	中譯	反義詞	中譯
Scene	*n.*	場面		
Unforgettable	*adj.*	無法忘懷的	Unremarkable	不值得注意的
Boiler	*n.*	鍋爐		
Reciprocate	*v.*	往復運動		
Perform	*v.*	執行	Abstain	避開
Mechanical	*adj.*	機械的	Manual	手動的
Fluid	*n.*	液體	Solid	固體的
Atmospheric	*adj.*	大氣中的	Grounded	地面上的
Effective	*adj.*	有效的	Ineffective	無效的
Beyond	*adv.*	深於		
Depth	*n.*	深度		
Piston	*n.*	活塞		
Continuous	*adj.*	連續的	Intermittent	間歇的
Rotary	*adj.*	旋轉的		
Force	*v.*	強迫	Leave alone	避免打擾

Thomas Newcomen

MP3 16

Thomas Newcomen was born in Dartmouth, Devon, England on February 24th 1664. He became an ironmonger and a Baptist lay preacher by calling. His ironmonger's business was greatly engaged with a mining business since it designed and offered tools to it. Since flooding in coal and tin mines was a major and frequent problem, Newcomen decided to create a machine that could help solve the problem. He created the first practical steam engine for water pumping which he got famous for.

The steam engine he created was developed in 1712. He got the idea from Thomas Savery and Denis Papin who also created a steam engine called "a fire engine". It is a kind of thermic syphon in which steam was admitted to an empty container and then condensed. The vacuum then sucked water from the bottom of the mine. However, this creation was not very effective and couldn't work beyond a limited depth of around thirty feet.

Newcomen inverted Savery's design and used a cylinder containing a piston based on Papin's design. It drew down the piston instead of vacuum drawing in water. The first successful engine was then created by Newcomen and his partner John Calley. Newcomen passed away in

01 Part 飲食民生

02 Part 歷史懷舊

03 Part 現代實用科技

04 Part 資訊知識

1729 at the age of 65 in London. Even so, the engine he created held its place without material change for about 75 years. It also spread gradually to more areas in UK and Europe.

湯馬仕・紐科

　　湯馬仕・紐科於 1664 年 2 月 24 日出生在英格蘭的德文郡，達特茅斯。他成為了一個鐵匠和浸禮會通過的佈道者。他的鐵匠業務與開礦業節節相關，因為他幫助設計和提供工具。由於洪水對於煤炭和錫礦業造成一個重要和常見的問題，紐科決定製作一個機器來幫助解決問題。他創造了第一個實用的蒸汽機來抽水，他也因此而成名。

　　他的蒸汽機是在 1712 年被開發出來。他是從由湯瑪士・薩弗里和丹尼斯・帕潘所創造，命名為「The Fire Engine」的蒸汽機所得到的想法。它是一種熱虹吸管，蒸氣在真空管中冷卻製造出空間，真空的吸管便可由礦底吸水。然而，這種創作不是很有效，無法在超出約三萬英尺的深度工作。

　　紐科倒置薩弗里的設計並使用含有帕潘設計的活塞氣缸。它在水中利用活塞來代替真空吸引。紐科和他的合夥人約翰・可雷因此創造了第一個成功的引擎。紐科去世於 1729 年倫敦，享年 65 歲。即便如此，他所創造的引擎在 75 年間都沒有重大的變化。它也逐漸蔓延到英國和歐洲的地區。

字彙

字彙	詞形	中譯	反義詞	中譯
Ironmonger	*n.*	五金商		
Preacher	*n.*	牧師		
Engage	*v.*	從事	Dismiss	解僱
Mining	*n.*	採礦		
Flood	*n.*	水災	Drought	旱災
Thermic	*adj.*	由熱造成的		
Syphon	*n.*	虹吸管		
Admit	*v.*	准許	Deny	拒絕
Condense	*v.*	壓縮	Extend	擴大
Invert	*v.*	反向	Right	正向
Cylinder	*n.*	汽缸		
Gradually	*adv.*	逐步地	Rapidly	迅速地

牛刀小試

1. The period when the Berlin Wall was torn down was an _____ experience.

   A. memorized   B. unforgettable
   C. interesting   D. unfortunate

2. After all their invitations, we should _____.

   A. receive   B. respond
   C. reciprocate   D. invite back

3. Exhaust from cars and factories, combined with _____ gases resulted in a thick layer of smog that might cause cancer.

   A. aromatic   B. atmospheric
   C. atomic   D. aeronautic

4. All organs require _____ supply of blood.

   A. concentrated   B. continue
   C. continuous   D. conceal

5. He was caught for _____ in the illegal drug trade.

   A. engaged
   B. engagement
   C. engaging
   D. engage

6. Sadly, the society still not widely _____ same sex marriage.

   A. approval
   B. agreed
   C. acceptable
   D. admit

7. Milk becomes _____ when water is taken out of it.

   A. concentrate
   B. shrunk
   C. reduce
   D. condensed

8. Due to the high humidity in Taiwan, after leaving the bicycle out in the rain for weeks, it _____ began to rust.

   A. instantly
   B. gradually
   C. slightly
   D. suddenly

題目解析

1. **(B)** 空白需填入形容詞,而由句意我們可以得知 unforgettable 是最適合的選項。表示柏林牆受到毀壞是個令人難忘的經驗。

2. **(C)** 由句意及字彙來看,reciprocate 是正確答案,表示在接受他們的邀請後,我們應該要回饋。

3. **(B)** 由字彙選擇,A 選項 aromatic, C 選項 atomic 和 D 選項 aeronautic 均不和句意故 atmospheric 為正確答案,表示汽車和工廠排放出的廢氣與大氣中的氣體結合,導致可能致癌的厚層煙霧。

4. **(C)** b 和 d 選項為動詞故可以先刪去,B 選項若改為 continued 可選,而 A 選項 concentrated 集中的不合句意。而由句意得知空格應填入「連續的」一詞,因此 continuous 為正確答案。

5. **(C)** Caught for 後面應加 v+ing,只有 c 選項符合故因此答案為 engaging,表示他因為違法毒品交易被捕。

6. **(D)** Widely 後面需加動詞 A 選項 approval 名詞,B 選項為分詞或過去式動詞,C 選項為形容詞均不符合,因此 admit 為正確答案,表示社會仍未廣泛地承認同性婚姻。。

7. **(D)** 空格需使用形容詞，因此解答為 condensed。Become, get 等連綴動詞其後須加入形容詞當補語而 A、B、C 均為動詞故均不選，意思是當水分從中抽取出後牛奶變得濃縮。

8. **(B)** 四個選項均為副詞但生鏽不會立即發生，所以解答為 gradually。

01
Part
飲食民生

02
Part
歷史懷舊

03
Part
現代實用科技

04
Part
資訊知識

Unit 09 9-1
Photographic Film
底片
by *George Eastman*

Photographic Film
MP3 17

Before digital photography became popular in the 21st century, photographic film was the dominant form of photography for hundreds of years. Without the invention of photographic film, movies would not be invented and many historical records would be much less realistic.

The first flexible photographic roll film was sold by George Eastman in 1885. It was a paper base film. In 1889, the first transparent plastic roll film was invented. It was made of cellulose nitrate which is chemically similar to guncotton. It was quite dangerous because it was highly flammable. Therefore, special storage was required. The first flexible movie films measured 35-mm wide and came in long rolls on a spool. Similar roll film for the camera was also invented in the mid 1920s. By the late 1920s, medium format roll film was created and had a paper backing which made it easy to handle in daylight.

Triacetate film came later and was more stable, flexible, and fireproof. This technology was widely used in the

1970s. Today, technology has produced film with T-grain emulsions. These films use light-sensitive silver halides (grains) that are T-shaped, thus rendering a much finer grain pattern. Films like this offer greater detail and higher resolution, meaning sharper images.

01
Part
飲食民生

02
Part
歷史懷舊

03
Part
現代實用科技

04
Part
資訊知識

底片

　　在 21 世紀數位攝影開始流行前，底片是攝影數百年來的主要形式。如果沒有底片的發明，電影將不會被發明，眾多的歷史記錄也會較不真實。

　　第一個柔性膠卷是由喬治・伊士曼於 1885 年售出。它是一種紙基膜。在 1889 年，第一個透明的塑料筒膜被發明出來。它是利用硝酸纖維素所製造，化學性質是類似於硝化纖維素。這其實是相當危險的，因為它是高度易燃的。因此，特殊的儲存方式是必要的。第一個柔性電影底片是 35 毫米寬，排列在長卷的捲筒上。相機類似的膠卷也在 1920 年代中期被發明出來。到了 1920 年代末期，中寬幅的底片被發明出來，它也有紙襯，使得它容易攜帶於日光下。

　　三醋酸纖維薄膜的膠卷後來被發明出來，它較為穩定、靈活和防火。這項技術於 1970 年代廣泛採用。今天，製造技術已經發展到 T 型顆粒乳劑。這些膜使用 T 型的光敏鹵化銀粒，使得圖像更為細緻。像這樣的底片提供了更多的細節和更高的解析度，這意味著更清晰的圖像。

字彙	詞形	中譯	反義詞	中譯
dominating	*adj.*	佔首位的	Minor	次要的
Historical	*adj.*	具歷史性的	Modern	現代的
Realistic	*adj.*	真實的	Unnatural	不自然的
Transparent	*adj.*	透明的	Opaque	不透光的
Guncotton	*n.*	棉火藥		
Flammable	*adj.*	易燃的	Fireproof	防火的
Storage	*n.*	保存		
Format	*n.*	形式		
Stable	*adj.*	穩定的	Undependable	不可依靠的
Emulsion	*n.*	感光劑		
Sensitive	*adj.*	敏感的	Insensitive	不敏感的
Render	*v.*	使得		
Resolution	*n.*	解析度		

George Eastman   MP3 18

George Eastman was born on July 12, 1854, in Waterville, New York. His father passed away when he was 8 and one of his sisters passed away when he was 16. Therefore, Eastman grew up very close with his mother and his another sister. As the son of the family, Eastman dropped out of school at the age of 14 to help with the

01
Part
飲食民生

02
Part
歷史懷舊

03
Part
現代實用科技

04
Part
資訊知識

family income.

At the age of 24, Eastman started his research on how to make photography less cumbersome and easy for people to enjoy. After a couple of years of research, Eastman launched his fledgling photography company in 1880. 5 years later, he patented a roll-holder device which allowed cameras to be smaller and cheaper. In 1888, he made the Kodak camera, which is the first camera designed specifically to use roll film. He also came up with the company slogan "You press the button; we do the rest." It is because the camera would be sent back to the company after the 100 exposures on the roll of film had been used up. Later Kodak would develop the pictures and send it back to the clients.

Eastman was not only a businessman, an inventor, but also an outstanding philanthropist. He was not stingy on sharing his fortune. In 1901, he donated $625,000 to Mechanics Institute which is the Rochester Institute of Technology today. He also helped the Massachusetts Institute of Technology to construct buildings on its second campus. He shared more of his fortune to establish educational and health institutions.

Unfortunately, in his later years, Eastman suffered from

an intense pain caused by a disorder which affected his spine. He was not able to stand or walk which effect greatly on his daily life. He decided to commit suicide and shot himself through his heart. He left a note which read, "To my friends, my work is done-why wait?" It was March 14th, 1932.

喬治・伊士曼

　　喬治・伊士曼於 1854 年 7 月 12 日出生於紐約，沃特維爾。他的父親在他 8 歲時去世。他的姊姊則是在他 16 歲時去世。因此，伊士曼在成長的過程中與他的媽媽和另一個姊姊的關係非常密切。作為家中的兒子，伊士曼在 14 歲時便輟學，以幫助家庭收入。

　　在 24 歲的時候，伊士曼開始了他對如何使攝影不太笨重，亦供人欣賞的研究。經過幾年的研究，伊士曼在 1880 年推出了他無經驗的攝影公司，並在 5 年以後，他獲得滾架裝置的專利，使相機更小、更便宜。1888 年，他做了第一台柯達攝影機，這是專門使用底片的第一台相機。他還提出了公司的口號「你按下按鈕；剩下的我們來做」。這是因為相機在用完 100 張底片後，會被送回柯達公司，之後柯達便會洗出相片，並將其寄送回客戶。

　　伊士曼不僅是一個商人，一個發明家，也是一位傑出的慈善家。他不吝嗇的分享他的財富。1901 年，他捐贈了 625,000 美元到力學研究所，也就是今天的羅切斯特技術學院。他還幫助美國麻省理工學院建立了其第二校舍。他分享了他更多的財富，建立教育和保健機構。

　　不幸的是，在伊士曼的晚年，他因為疾病造成了他脊椎的劇烈疼痛。他不能站立或行走，顯著的影響了他的生活。他決定朝他的心臟開槍自殺。他留了張紙條，上面寫著「給我的朋友，我完成了我的工作，何需等待。」這是 1932 年 3 月 14 日。

必考字彙表

字彙	詞形	中譯	反義詞	中譯
Cumbersome	*adj.*	笨重的	Manageable	易操縱的
Launch	*v.*	開始從事	Close	關閉
Fledge	*v.*	小鳥長羽毛		
Device	*n.*	裝置		
Specifically	*adv.*	特別地	Vaguely	模糊的
Slogan	*n.*	標語		
Exposure	*n.*	暴露	Concealment	隱藏
Outstanding	*adj.*	傑出的	Abysmal	極壞的
Philanthropist	*n.*	慈善家	Misanthropist	厭世者
Stingy	*adj.*	吝嗇的	Generous	慷慨的
Donate	*v.*	捐贈		
Institute	*n.*	學會		
Establish	*v.*	建立	Close down	關閉
Suffer	*v.*	忍受	Relieve	緩和
Disorder	*n.*	失調	Systematize	系統化

9-2 試題演練

牛刀小試

1. China has _____ the world champion for table tennis and badminton for decades.

   A. carrying   B. dominated
   C. placed   D. stand

2. As long as you set _____ goals for yourself and keep up with the study plan, it will be a piece of cake to enter the school you desired.

   A. unrealistic   B. dreamy
   C. imaginable   D. realistic

3. Some insects have _____ wings that you can see the veins running thru them.

   A. rough   B. opaque
   C. transformative   D. transparent

4. Infants are very _____ to the temperature change, so it is important to keep the room temperature steady.

A. responsible   B. sensitive

C. resilient   D. numb

5. The camera _____ on an iPhone is even better than some digital cameras now, which made people stop carrying digital cameras while traveling these days.

A. revolution   B. renovation

C. resolution   D. recapitulation

6. X-ray machines emit radiation, so _____ should be limited.

A. exposure   B. disclose

C. reveal   D. cover

7. Being a _____, she contributes most of her money and time to a local orphan center.

A. philosopher   B. psychiatrist

C. philanthropist   D. psychologist

8. The famous singer Karen Carpenter had anorexia, which is a potentially life-threatening eating _____ that is characterized by an intense fear of gaining weight. She eventually starved herself to death.

A. systematize   B. disease

C. cycle   D. disorder

01 Part 飲食民生

02 Part 歷史懷舊

03 Part 現代實用科技

04 Part 資訊知識

題目解析

1. **(B)** has 後面應加 v＋ed，又由句意得知 dominated 為正確解答表示中國在這幾十年來，佔據了桌球和羽球世界盃的頭銜。

2. **(D)** 由句意及字彙可清楚得知 realistic 為正確答案，表示只要你替自己設定實際的目標，且持續趕上這個學習計劃，你將發現進理想中學校是輕而易舉的。

3. **(D)** 後半句中說明了可看見 veins running thru，因此得知空格應選 transparent。

4. **(B)** 由句意可得知「敏感」是最適合的字彙，因此 sensitive 為正確解答。表示嬰兒對溫度改變是敏感的，所以保持室溫的穩定是重要的，其中 be sensitive to 為常考用法。

5. **(C)** 相機的解析度即為 resolution，所以答案為 resolution。表示 iPhone 的相機解析度甚至比有些數位相機高，使得人們於這些日子旅行時，不攜帶數位相機了。

6. **(A)** 空格應填入名詞，因此解答為 exposure。

7. **(C)** 由句意可得知「慈善家」是最適合的字彙，因此解答為 philanthropist 表示身為一個慈善家，她貢獻大部分她的金錢和時間給當地一間嬰兒中心。

8. (D) 厭食症的英文為 eating disorder，因此解答為 disorder。不管是單字題或於閱讀題中，許多字詞常有 paraphrase，以另一個方式表達字義，eating disorder 即是 anoxeria 的另一個同義表達。

Unit 10　10-1
Paper
紙

by *Cai Lun*

 **Paper** MP3 19

Before paper was invented, several materials such as papyrus, parchment, palm leaves and vellum were being used as written materials, but they were all expensive and limited. Paper was invented by Cai Lun, an official of the Imperial Court, in 105 A.D. in China during the Han Dynasty. He broke the bark of a mulberry tree into fibers and added in rags hemp and old fish nets which created the first piece of paper. He reported to the emperor and received great honor for his ability. Because of this invention, paper can be produced with trees at a vey low cost, which popularized the use of paper. In a few years, paper was widely used in China.

Even though Chinese invented paper in 105 A.D., invented printing technology at around 600 A.D., and printed the first newspaper by 740 A.D., this amazing technology was only spread to the eastern countries including Korea and Japan at as early as the 6th century. The paper making technique was brought to the western countries along the Silk Road. The technique was found at Tibet at around 650

A.D.

China used to be a closed country. For a long time, the Chinese kept the paper manufacture as a secret to ensure a monopoly. However, losing in a battle at the Talas River, the Chinese prisoners revealed the paper making technique to the Arabs which helped them built the first paper industry in Baghdad in 793 A.D. Interestingly, the Arabs also kept the first technique as a secret from the European. As a result, the paper making technique did not reach Europe until hundreds of years later. Spain built the first European paper factory in 1150 A.D. Finally, after another 500 years, the first paper industry was built in Philadelphia in the USA. That is 1500 years after the first piece of paper was made!

紙

在造紙術發明前，紙莎草、羊皮紙、棕櫚葉和上等紙都被用作書面材料，但他們都價格昂貴而且供給有限。紙是在公元 105 年，在中國漢朝由一位朝廷的官員蔡倫所發明的。他打碎了桑樹的樹皮做為纖維，在裡面加入了碎布麻與舊漁網，製造了第一張紙。他向皇帝報告，並因此受到了極大的榮譽。因為這個發明，紙就可以利用樹生產低成本的紙，使紙被廣為利用 。在短短幾年內，紙被廣泛應用於中國。

儘管中國人在公元 105 年發明了紙，在公元 600 年發明了印刷技術，並在公元 **740** 年打印了首次的報紙，這個驚人的技術卻到第六世紀時傳播到東方國家，包括韓國和日本。造紙技術因為絲綢之路被帶到了西方國家。該技術約在公元 **650** 年左右在西藏被發現。

中國曾經是一個封閉的國家。長期以來，中國一直將造紙技術保密，以確保壟斷。然而公元 **793** 年，由於在失去塔拉斯河的戰役，中國戰俘透露製作技術並幫助阿拉伯人在巴格達建立了第一個造紙行業。有意思的是，阿拉伯人也將此技術保密。因此，造紙技術在幾百年後才傳到歐洲。西班牙在公元 **1150** 年時建立了第一個歐洲的造紙廠，再過 **500** 年後美國的費城才建立了美國的第一個造紙廠。這是從第一張紙被發明算起的 **1500** 年後！

必考字彙表

字彙	詞性	中譯	反義詞	中譯
Papyrus	*n.*	紙莎草		
Parchment	*n.*	羊皮紙		
Vellum	*n.*	羊皮紙		
Official	*n.*	官員	Employee	僱員
Imperial	*adj.*	帝國的	Common	一般的
Bark	*n.*	樹皮	Core	果核
Fiber	*n.*	纖維		
Hemp	*n.*	麻		
Emperor	*n.*	皇帝	Empress	皇后
Honor	*n.*	榮譽	Disgrace	恥辱
Ability	*n.*	能力	Incompetence	無能

Spread	*v.*	使延伸	Compress	壓縮
Manufacture	*v.*	製造	Destroy	毀壞
Ensure	*v.*	保證	Deny	否認
Battle	*n.*	戰役	Harmony	和睦
Reveal	*v.*	展露出	Conceal	隱瞞

Around 2000 years ago, Cai Lun was born in Guiyang during the Han Dynasty. Because of his father's accusation, Cai was brought to the palace and got castrated at the age of 12. Even so, Cai loved to study and was designated to study along with the Emperor's son. He was a very hard working person , so he was given several promotions under the role of Emperor He. He was given the right to be in charged of manufacturing instruments and weapons. Later on, he was promoted to become a Regular Palace Attendant which is known as the staff officer now. He was in charged of everything being produced for the palace which started his thought on a papermaking process. Cai was given recognition for his invention of paper and named as one of the greatest inventors of China until now.

As loyal as he was, Cai unfortunately was ordered to report to prison after Emperor An assumed power. Cai was

01
Part
飲食民生

02
Part
歷史懷舊

03
Part
現代實用科技

04
Part
資訊知識

rogued to frame the grandmother of Emperor An. He felt greatly insulted, so before he was to report, he committed suicide by drinking poison. Hundreds of years later at Song Dynasty, a temple in honor of Cai Lun had been erected in Chengdu. Nowadays, people in the paper business travels long distance to pay respect.

蔡倫

大約 2000 多年前，蔡倫出生於漢朝的貴陽。由於他的父親犯罪，因此蔡被帶到了皇宮，在 12 歲時便被閹割。即便如此，蔡倫喜愛學習，所以被指定當作皇帝兒子的陪讀。他是一個很努力工作的人，因此在漢和帝的執政下被多次的升官。他被任命負責儀器及武器的製作。後來，他被晉升中常侍，即是現在的參謀。他負責宮中一切物品的製作。這開始了他造紙過程的想法。由於紙的發明，蔡倫受到認可且直到現在都被認為是中國最偉大的發明家之一。

忠誠的他在漢安帝上位後指派入獄。原因是蔡倫被誣告陷害皇帝的祖母。他感到極大的侮辱，因此在他需要向監獄報到前，蔡倫服毒自殺。幾百年後，在宋朝，紀念蔡倫的廟宇被建立在成都。如今，從事紙類商務的人們仍長途旅行以瞻仰蔡倫。

字彙

字彙	詞形	中譯	反義詞	中譯
Dynasty	*n.*	朝代		
Accusation	*n.*	控告	Commendation	表揚
Palace	*n.*	皇宮		
Castrate	*v.*	閹割	Remain	留下
Designate	*v.*	指派	Disallow	駁回
Promotion	*n.*	晉級	Demotion	降級
Weapon	*n.*	武器		
Attendant	*n.*	侍從	Manager	主管
Process	*n.*	製作	Cessation	中斷
Recognition	*n.*	表揚	Blame	責備
Assume	*v.*	取得	Release	釋放
Rogue	*v.*	欺騙		
Frame	*v.*	陷害		
Insult	*v.*	侮辱	Praise	稱讚
Commit suicide		自殺		

10-2 試題演練

牛刀小試

1. It is an _____ to receive the Employee of the Year award.

   A. pride
   B. honor
   C. proud
   D. successful

2. She is the employee with the most considerable _____.

   A. ability
   B. knowhow
   C. abilities
   D. knowhows

3. The government's responsibility is to _____ citizens' happiness.

   A. make sure
   B. sure
   C. ensure
   D. unsure

4. All candidates are required to _____ his or her family fortune in order to enter the election.

   A. donate
   B. give up
   C. reveal
   D. hidden

5. Customer services are required to make reports when receive _____ for bad services.

   A. letter   B. suggestion

   C. accusation   D. request

6. This area of the park has been specially _____ for children.

   A. designated   B. signed

   C. circled   D. marked

7. Many small countries are hard to gain diplomatic _____ from the international community.

   A. understanding   B. friendship

   C. recognition   D. relation

8. It is against the company rules to make any _____ about other's appearance.

   A. comments   B. compliments

   C. suggestions   D. insults

01 Part 飲食民生

02 Part 歷史懷舊

03 Part 現代實用科技

04 Part 資訊知識

1. (B) 此空格應填入名詞，c 和 d 為形容詞故可先刪去，且由句意及字詞可以了解 honor 為正確解答。

2. (C) 由 the most 可以揣測此處應填入複數名詞，而由字意我們可以選出 abilities 為正確選項。

3. (C) 4 個選項均為 sure 的變化形。而此處應填入有「擔保」意味的動詞，因此解答為 ensure。Make sure 其後加 that 子句，若其後改成 make sure that every citizen is happy 可選 make sure。

4. (C) 選項 a 和 b 為形容詞故可先刪去，由句意及字詞可以簡單選出答案為 reveal。

5. (C) 此空格應填入名詞，而由最後兩個字 bad services 可以猜測到解答為 accusation。

6. (A) 雖說 circled 跟 marked 似乎也可以用在這個地方，但以英語的通用來看，designated 還是最恰當的答案。相似的用法有 be specifically tailored to…為…量身訂做的。

7. (C) 此空格應填入名詞，而由句意可以挑選出 recognition 為正確解答。

8. **(D)** 由句意可以理解這裡應選擇有關形容外觀的負面名詞，因此答案為 insults。

01
Part
飲食民生

02
Part
歷史懷舊

03
Part
現代實用科技

04
Part
資訊知識

Unit 11 11-1
Liquid Paper
立可白
by *Bette Graham*

💡 Liquid Paper

MP3 21

The sales of liquid paper dropped dramatically in recent decade. However, back in the late 90th while computers were not as common, liquid paper could be found in every pen case and on every desk. Where did the name liquid paper come from? It is actually a brand name of the Newell Rubbermaid company that sells correction products.

It is not a surprise that liquid paper was invented by a typist. Bette Graham who used to make many mistakes while working as a typist, invented the first correction fluid in her kitchen back in 1951. Using only paints and kitchen ware, Graham made her first generation correction fluid called Mistake Out and started to sell it to her co-workers. Graham for sure saw the business opportunity with her invention and founded the Mistake Out Company back in 1956 while she was still working as a typist. However, she was later on fired from her job because of some silly mistakes. Just like that, she worked from her kitchen alone for 17 years. At 1961, the company name was changed to Liquid Paper and it was sold to the Gillette Corporation for

$47.5 million in 1979. Who would have thought!

Even though liquid paper was so convenient and popular, everyone who used liquid paper before knows that it has a funky smell. It is because it contains titanium dioxide, solvent naphtha, mineral spirits and also trichloroethane which later on were found to be toxic. Since it affects human body, fewer and fewer people use liquid paper. Instead of fluid, a later invention by the same company, correction tape, is getting more popular these days. What will come next? Let's wait and see.

立可白

立可白在近幾十年的銷售急劇下降。然而在九零年代，當電腦還不普及時，你幾乎可以在每一個鉛筆盒，每一張桌子上看到立可白。立可白這個名字究竟是從何而來？ 它實際上是 Newell Rubbermaid 公司所銷售之修正產品的品牌名稱。

立可白是由一位打字員所發明的，這並不意外。貝蒂‧格雷厄姆在當打字員時經常發生錯誤。因此，在 1951 年時格雷厄姆在她的廚房裡，只利用了油漆及廚具，發明了她的第一代修正液，並且將它賣給自己的同事。格雷厄姆肯定看到了這個發明的商機，在 1956 年她還在擔任打字員時便創辦了 Mistake Out 公司。爾後，她因為一些愚蠢的原因被公司解雇。就這樣，她在廚房裡獨自工作了 17 年。在 1961 年，

01
Part
飲食民生

02
Part
歷史懷舊

03
Part
現代實用科技

04
Part
資訊知識

該公司的名稱改為立可白，並在 1979 年以 $47.5 百萬美元出售給吉列特公司。誰會想到！

　　儘管立可白是如此的方便和流行，每個使用過立可白的人都知道它有一個特殊的氣味。這是因為它包含二氧化鈦、溶劑石腦油、礦油精和之後被發現是有毒的三氯乙烷。由於它影響人類的身體，因此越來越少的人使用立可白。取代液態式的修正液，由同一家公司所發明的修正帶越來越趨於流行。接下來還會有什麼發明呢？讓我們拭目以待。

必考字彙表

字彙	詞性	中譯	反義詞	中譯
Drop	v.	下降	Rise	上升
Dramatically	adv.	戲劇性的	Naturally	自然的
Decade	n.	十年		
Common	adj.	普通的	Particular	特殊的
Correction	n.	校正	Damage	損害
Typist	n.	打字員		
Ware	n.	器具		
Generation	n.	世代	Destruction	毀滅
Opportunity	n.	機會	Misfortune	厄運
Convenient	adj.	便利的	Inexpedient	不適當的
Funky	adj.	惡臭的	Aroma	香氣
Contain	v.	包含	Exclude	不包含
Mineral	n.	礦物		
Toxic	adj.	有毒的	Wholesome	有益健康的

 Bette Graham MP3 22

A half a million-dollar business owner, an artist, an inventor, and a single mother, Bette Graham was an independent woman with multiple successful roles in her life. Graham was born Bette Clair McMurray in Dallas, Texas in 1924. She got married and had her only one child Robert Michael Nesmith in 1942. In 1946, she filed in her first divorce. She raised her child alone and got married again to Robert Graham in 1962. Unfortunately, the marriage didn't last, and they were divorced in 1975.

As an artist, Graham had a special talent in painting. Aside from being the typist, she used to paint holiday windows for banks to earn extra money. She said that she realized that with lettering, an artist never corrects by erasing, but always paints over the error. That's her million-dollar idea! Graham made her first correction fluid in her kitchen and secretly she began marketing it as Mistake Out. Soon after she began her company, she changed the name yet again to Liquid Paper which became well-known by the popularity.

Graham was a brilliant woman who ran her business in a unique way. She believed in quality over profit which brought her the half a million-dollar business. She also believed that women could bring more humanistic quality to the male world of business. Therefore, she started an employee library and a childcare center in her new company headquarters in 1975. Her steps were followed by many international corporations these days. Bette Graham should not only be known as the inventor of Liquid Paper but should be called as the employee benefit creator.

貝蒂‧格雷厄姆

　　擁有價值 50 萬美元的企業家、藝術家、發明家和一個單身母親，貝蒂‧格雷厄姆是一個在生活中擁有多個成功角色的獨立女人。格雷厄姆的原名為貝蒂‧克萊爾‧麥克默里，於 1924 年出生於德州的達拉斯。她在 1942 年結了婚，並有了她唯一的孩子羅伯特‧邁克爾‧奈史密斯。1946 年，她申請了第一次的離婚。她獨自扶養她的孩子，並且在 1962 年嫁給了羅伯特‧格雷厄姆。不幸的是，婚姻並沒有持續多久，他們在 1975 年離婚。

　　作為一個藝術家，格雷厄姆是個繪畫天才。從事打字員外，她利用假日油漆銀行的櫥窗來賺外快。她說當時她意識到，就刻字來說，藝術家從不刪除錯誤而是利用描繪掩蓋錯誤。這可是她價值數百萬美元的主！格雷厄姆在她的廚房裡做了她第一代的塗改液並爾後她偷偷地開始了營銷 Mistake Out。在她成立公司後不久，她再次將產品更名為廣受人知的立可白。

　　格雷厄姆是一個以獨特的方式做生意的聰明女性。她相信品質比利潤重要，這個想法帶給了她超過五十萬美元的營業利潤。她還認為，女性更可以在這個以男性為主的企業社會裡帶來更多的人文素養。因此在 1975 年，她在她的新公司總部開始了員工圖書館和托兒中心。她的腳步在近期內被許多跨國公司相繼跟進。貝蒂·格雷厄姆不僅應該被稱為立可白的發明者，更應該被稱為員工福利的創造者。

必考字彙表

字彙	詞性	中譯	反義詞	中譯
Independent	*adj.*	獨立的	Dependent	依賴的
Multiple	*adj.*	複合的	Single	單一的
Divorce	*v.*	離婚	Marriage	婚姻
Unfortunately	*adv.*	不幸地	Luckily	幸運地
Talent	*n.*	資質	Inability	無能
Lettering	*n.*	寫字		
Error	*n.*	錯誤	Accuracy	準確性
Eventually	*adv.*	最後	Immediately	立即地
Marketing	*n.*	行銷		
Brilliant	*adj.*	傑出的	Dulled	乏味的
Unique	*adj.*	獨特的	Common	一般的
Humanistic	*adj.*	人道主義的	Inhuman	無人性的
Childcare	*n.*	兒童照顧		
Headquarter	*n.*	總部		

11-2 試題演練

牛刀小試

1. Your life will change _____ after you have a newborn.

    A. small   B. dramatic

    C. similar   D. dramatically

2. Mary was told to re-do all the math questions that were return with _____.

    A. circle   B. error

    C. correct   D. corrections

3. It is our responsibility to preserve the planet for the future _____.

    A. generation   B. people

    C. generations   D. person

4. It is important to take healthy meals with all necessary vitamins and _____.

    A. liquid   B. minerals

    C. element   D. protein

5. Supermarkets provide _____ household supplies.

   A. very   B. much

   C. multiple   D. single

6. _____, we missed the train by 5 minutes, and now we have to delay all our schedules.

   A. Fortunate   B. Unfortunate

   C. Fortunately   D. Unfortunately

7. Ellen DeGeneres wins her career with her _____ sense of humor.

   A. marvelous   B. brilliant

   C. doubtful   D. controversial

8. Due to her belief in _____, she forces her employees to work no more than 8 hours a day.

   A. law   B. labor

   C. humanistic   D. union

01 Part 飲食民生

02 Part 歷史懷舊

03 Part 現代實用科技

04 Part 資訊知識

題目解析

1. (D) a, b 和 c 為形容詞故可先刪去，此空格應該填入形容動詞 change 的副詞，因此解答為 dramatically。

2. (D) 由句意及字詞可以挑選出 corrections 為正確解答。另一個簡單的選擇方式為 all the math question's」為複數，因此空格應該也須選擇複數的答案，即為 corrections。

3. (C) 由句意及字詞可以挑選出 generation 為正確詞彙，然而我們需要為的是以後的多個世代，並非單一個世代，因此應挑選複數 generations。

4. (B) Liquid 及 protein 皆不足形容我們所需的營養，而 element 並非我們所攝取的物質，因此礦物質 minerals 為正確解答。Minerals 和 vitamins 為常見搭配。

5. (C) 超市所提供的是可數的「多樣」物品，因此 multiple 為正確解答。

6. (D) a 和 b 為形容詞故可先刪去，且副詞放在句首可以有強調語句的效果，因此應選 c 或 d。而由句意可以了解 unfortunately 為正確解答。

7. (B) 此空格應放入形容 sense of humor 的形容詞，前句的 wins her career 有闡明是正面的形容詞，故刪掉選項 c 和 d，因此 brilliant 為正確解答。

8. (C) 此題由後句選出 humanistic 為正確解答。

01
Part
飲食民生

02
Part
歷史懷舊

03
Part
現代實用科技

04
Part
資訊知識

Unit 12 12-1
Ballpoint Pen
原子筆
by *John Jacob Loud*

Ballpoint Pen MP3 23

A seemingly simple concept and an easy invention, ballpoint pens were developed in the late 19th century. The first patent for a ballpoint pen was issued to John J. Load in October 1888. The idea was to design a writing instrument that would be able to write on rough surfaces such as wood which fountain pens could not. Unfortunately, the potential was not seen and the ink technology was not reliable enough to make the ballpoint pen commercially available. The ink was either too thick or too thin which caused overflowing or clogging problems.

Until 1938, a Hungarian newspaper editor Laszlo Biro was smart enough to use newspaper ink for pen since newspaper ink dried quickly and was smudge free However, news paper ink dried too fast to be held in the reservoir. Luckily, his brother Gyorgy, a chemist, developed viscous ink formulas for the ball point pens which compatibly prevent ink from drying inside the reservoir while allowing controlled flow. The Biro brothers later on filed a new patent in 1943 with their friend Juan Jorge Meyne and started to manufacture the Birome Pens in Argentina.

The Birome was brought to the United States in 1945 by a mechanical pencil maker, Eversharp Co. Eversharp Co. and Eberhard Faner Co. teamed up and licensed the rights to sell the Birome ballpoint pen in the US. At the same time, an American entrepreneur Milton Reynolds saw the potential of ballpoint pen, and therefore founded the Reynolds International Pen Company. Both companies were doing great and ballpoint pen sales went rocket high in 1946, though people were still not 100% satisfied. Another famous ballpoint pen maker would be Marcel Bich. Bich was the founder of the famous pen company Bic we all recognize today. The Bic ballpoint pen has the history since 1953.

01
Part
飲食民生

02
Part
歷史懷舊

03
Part
現代實用科技

04
Part
資訊知識

原子筆

　　原子筆，看似一個簡單的概念和發明，是在 19 世紀後期被開發出來的。但其實它並不如你認為的如此容易。原子筆的第一個專利是在 1888 年 10 月由約翰‧勞德所取得。他一開始的想法是設計一個能在粗糙表面，如木頭，上書寫的工具。這是鋼筆做不到的。不幸的是由於時機未到且油墨的技術還不夠可靠到能將原子筆市售。當時的油墨不是太濃稠就是太稀，因而造成油墨溢出或阻塞的問題。

直到1938年，匈牙利報紙拉斯洛‧比羅很聰明的想到利用報紙油墨作為筆的墨水，因為報紙的印刷油墨快乾，且沒有暈染的問題。但他面臨了另一個問題。報紙的油墨乾燥過快，無法存放在筆芯中。幸運的是，他的弟弟捷爾吉是位化學家，他發明初粘性不同的油墨配方，可放於原子筆的筆芯中，在防止乾涸的同時有能控制流量。 比羅兄弟後來與他們的朋友胡安‧豪爾赫 美恩 在 1943 年時提出新的專利，並開始在阿根廷製造 Birome 原子筆。

　　Birome 原子筆在 1945 年由自動鉛筆公司 Eversharp 公司聯合 Eberhard Faner 公司拿下特許權，並在美國販售 Birome 原子筆。在同時，美國企業家米爾頓‧雷諾茲看到原子筆的潛力，並因此成立了雷諾國際製筆公司。兩家公司都在做得非常好，原子筆銷量在 1946 年到達高峰，雖然人們仍然不是 100%滿意。另一個著名的圓珠筆製造商是馬塞爾‧畢克。畢克是著名的筆公司 Bic 的創辦人。Bic 原子筆擁有自 1953 年以來的歷史。

必考字彙表

字彙	詞形	中譯	反義詞	中譯
Instrument	*n.*	器具		
Surface	*n.*	表面	Inner	內部
Fountain pen	*n.*	鋼筆		
Reliable	*adj.*	可靠的	Undependable	不可靠的
Overflow	*v.*	溢出	Dehydrate	缺水
Clog	*v.*	堵塞	Unblock	除去障礙

Editor	*n.*	編輯		
Smudge	*v.*	玷污	Purify	淨化
Reservoir	*n.*	儲存器		
Compatibly	*adj.*	相容的	Incompatible	不相容的
Flow	*v.*	流動	Conceal	隱瞞
Mechanical	*adj.*	機械的	Manual	手動的
Entrepreneur	*n.*	企業家	Employee	員工
Satisfied	*adj.*	感到滿意的	Dissatisfied	不滿的
Recognize	*v.*	表彰	Deny	否認

01
Part
飲食民生

02
Part
歷史懷舊

03
Part
現代實用科技

04
Part
資訊知識

John Jacob Loud MP3 24

Unlike most inventors, whose inventions were appreciated by the society when they were alive, John Jacob Loud did not.

As a very smart kid, he later graduated from Harvard College, but instead of becoming a lawyer, Loud followed his father's step and became a loyal cashier at the Union National Bank. He remained at his job for over 20 years until his resignation in 1895 for health reasons.

Loud obtained the first patent for ballpoint pen in 1888. The idea was to use a tiny steel ball as tip of the pen and make a writing instrument that can be used on leather products, which fountain pens could not. He noted in the patent: My invention consists of an improved reservoir or fountain pen, especially useful, among other purposes, for marking on rough surfaces-such as wood, coarse wrapping-paper, and other articles where an ordinary pen could not be used." However, the potential of ballpoint pen went unexploited because it was too coarse for letter writing. It was not until viscous ink formulas were developed did ballpoint pen become popular, about 27 years after Loud passed away.

約翰‧雅各‧勞德

與大多數發明家不同的是，約翰勞德於生前的發明並未受到社會重視。身為一個聰明的小孩，他之後於哈佛學院畢業，追隨父親的腳步成為國家聯邦銀行一個忠實的出納員，而不是律師。

勞德在 1888 年獲得的第一個原字筆的專利。當時的想法是利用一個小鋼球作為筆尖，使書寫工具可以用在皮革製品上。這是當時鋼筆所不能做到的。他在該專利中指出：我的發明包括一種改進的貯存器，使鋼筆有特別用途，可用於標記在粗糙表面上，如木材、粗包裝紙，和其它製品。這是一般筆所做不到的。然而，原子筆的潛力未被開發，因為設計的過於粗糙，無法使用於書信中。直到開發出油墨配方，原子筆才走紅，大約是勞德死後的27年了。

字彙

字彙	詞形	中譯	反義詞	中譯
Appreciate	*v.*	讚賞	Depreciate	貶低
Society	*n.*	社會		
Alive	*adj.*	活著的	Dead	死的
Instead	*adj.*	作為代替		
Follow	*v.*	跟隨	Lead	領導
Cashier	*n.*	出納員		
Loyal	*adj.*	忠誠的	Faithless	不忠誠的
Remain	*v.*	保持		
Resignation	*n.*	辭職		
Obtain	*v.*	取得	Lose	失去
Tiny	*adj.*	非常小的	Enormous	巨大的
Consist	*v.*	構成		
Improve	*v.*	改進	Descent	墮落
Coarse	*adj.*	粗的	Smooth	平滑的
Ordinary	*adj.*	普通的	Extraordinary	非凡的
Viscous	*adj.*	黏稠的	Runny	水份過多的

01
Part
飲食民生

02
Part
歷史懷舊

03
Part
現代實用科技

04
Part
資訊知識

12-2 試題演練

牛刀小試

1. Airplanes are the most _____ form of commercial transportation.

   A. reasonable   B. comfortable

   C. convenient   D. reliable

2. Unfortunately, the software I bought yesterday is not _____ with my computer.

   A. reliable   B. suitable

   C. convertible   D. compatible

3. The captain just announced that the plane couldn't take off due to a _____ problem.

   A. manual   B. machine

   C. mechanical   D. manpower

4. The puppy had been missing for 6 months, but she still _____ her family when they found her in the shelter.

A. realized   B. forgot
C. recognized   D. know

5. We must not _____ the work a kid has done.

   A. recognize   B. appreciate
   C. discover   D. depreciate

6. 12 years ago, there was a calling for the immediate _____ of the President in Taiwan.

   A. leave   B. resignation
   C. abandon   D. rejection

7. The team is confident of winning the world champion because it _____ of the best players from all over the country.

   A. consists   B. competes
   C. conducts   D. contaminates

8. Many people still don't have the _____ of time even though they are not kids anymore.

   A. thinking   B. thought
   C. concern   D. concept

1. (D) 選擇題的四個形容詞中最適當的答案為 reliable。表示飛機是最可靠的商業運輸形式。

2. (D) 由文句中我們了解應該選擇「可對應的」一詞，因此答案為 compatible。表示很不幸地是，我昨天買的軟體與我的電腦不相容，Be compatible with 表示…與…相對應或相容而 be suitable for 表示...適合，介係詞是用 for。

3. (C) 空白處應填入使飛機無法起飛的形容詞。因此最適當的答案為 mechanical，表示機長宣布飛機因為機械問題而無法起飛。

4. (C) 此句為過去式的敘述，因此 d 可以先刪除。又由句意可以了解 recognized 為正確答案。

5. (D) Must NOT 是關鍵。Not 後不可能在選句正面意思的詞像是 appreciate，且依句意 depreciate 是正確答案，表示我們不該貶低孩子所完成的事。

6. (B) 由文句得知空格應填入「辭職」一詞，因此答案為 resignation。表示 12 年前，有個立即要台灣總統下台的呼籲。

7. (A) 此處需填入動詞，並由句意可推測 consists 為正確解答。Consist of 為…由…組成的。

8. (D) 此處需填入名詞，並由句意可推測 concept 最為恰當，且 the concept of time 表示時間觀念，整句的意思是許多人仍沒有時間觀念，儘管他們不是小孩子了。

01
Part
飲食民生

02
Part
歷史懷舊

03
Part
現代實用科技

04
Part
資訊知識

Unit 13 13-1
Pencil
鉛筆
by **Nicolas Jacques Conte**

Pencil MP3 25

Back in ancient Roman, scribes used a thin metal rod called a "stylus" to leave readable mark on papyrus. Styluses were made of lead which we call pencil core now. Although, pencil cores now are no longer made with lead but non-toxic graphite. In 1564, a large graphite deposit in Borrowdale, England. The graphite could leave much darker mark than lead which is more suitable to be used as stylus, but the material was much softer and was hard to hold. Nicolas-Jacques Conte, a French painter, invented the modern pencil lead at the request of Lazare Nicolas Marguerite Carnot. Conte mixed powdered graphite with clay and pressing the material between two half-cylinders of wood. Thus was formed the modern pencil. Conte received a patent for the invention in 1795.

During the 19th century industrial revolution, started by Faber-Castell, Lyra and other companies, pencil industry was very active. United States used to import pencils from Europe until the war with England which cut off imports. In 1812, a Massachusetts cabinet maker, William Monroe, made the first wooden pencil. The American pencil industry also took off during the 19th century. Starting with the Joseph Dixon Crucible Company, many pencil factories are based on the East Coast , such as New York or New Jersey.

At first, pencils were all natural, unpainted and without printing company's names. Not until 1890s, many pencil companies started to paint pencils in yellow and put their brand name on it.

"Why yellow? Red or blue would look nice, too." You might think. It was actually a special way to tell the consumer that the graphite came from China. It is because back in the 1800's, the best graphite in the world came from China. And the color yellow in China means royalty and respect. Only the imperial family is allowed to use color yellow. Therefore, the American pencil companies began to paint their pencils bright yellow to show the regal feeling.

鉛筆

　　早在古羅馬，文士用細金屬絲作成「手寫筆」在莎草紙上留下可讀的標誌。手寫筆是由鉛所製造，我們現在也稱之為鉛筆芯。雖然，鉛筆芯已經不再是由鉛製成而是由無毒的石墨製成。 1564 年在英格蘭博羅發現了大型的石墨礦床。石墨可以留下比鉛更深的標記，但該物質更柔軟並且難用手握。尼古拉斯・雅克・孔特，一個法國畫家，依照拉扎爾尼古拉斯・瑪格麗特卡諾的要求，發明了鉛筆。孔特混合粉狀石墨和粘土，並在兩個半圓柱木材的材料上施壓。由此形成了現代鉛筆。孔特在 1795 年獲得了專利。

在 19 世紀的工業革命，輝柏嘉、天琴座等公司為開端，鉛筆行業非常活躍。美國使用從歐洲進口的鉛筆，直到與英國的戰爭，切斷了進口。 1812 年，麻省的一個櫥櫃製造商，威廉・莫瑞，製作了第一個木製鉛筆。美國製筆業也是在 19 世紀起飛。由約瑟夫・狄克遜公司開始，很多鉛筆工廠都開在東岸，如紐約或新澤西州。起初，鉛筆都是天然的，沒有油漆，沒有印刷公司的名稱。直到 1890 年代，許多鉛筆公司開始把鉛筆漆成黃色，並把自己的品牌名稱印上。

你可能會認為「為什麼是黃色？紅色或藍色的也很好看。」。它實際上是用一種特殊的方式在告訴大家，石墨是來自中國。這是因為早在 1800 年時，世界上最好的石墨來自中國。而在中國，黃色意味著皇室和尊重。只有皇室允許使用的黃色。因此，美國的鉛筆公司開始將自己的鉛筆漆成明亮的黃色，以顯示帝王的感覺。

必考字彙表

字彙	詞性	中譯	反義詞	中譯
Ancient	*adj.*	古代的	Modern	現代的
Core	*n.*	芯	Exterior	表面的
Toxic	*adj.*	有毒的	Harmless	無害的

Graphite	*n.*	石墨		
Suitable	*adj.*	適合的	Awkward	不合適的
Half-cylinder		半圓柱		
Active	*adj.*	活躍的	Inactive	不活躍的
Cabinet	*n.*	櫥櫃		
Royalty	*n.*	王室	Subservience	卑屈
Respect	*v.*	敬重	Disrespect	無禮的
Regal	*adj.*	帝王的	Common	普通的

Nicolas-Jacques Conte MP3 26

Here we will be introducing Nicolas Jacques Conte who was credited as the inventor of the modern lead pencil from France. Born in 1755, Conte was not only an inventor but also a painter, chemist, physicist, engineer and even scientist. Very different from the invention of pencil, Conte also has the reputation as an expert in balloon warfare which ensured his inclusion in the party of some 200 academics and scientists to accompany Napoleon on his expedition to Egypt in 1798. Unfortunately, the event ended as a disaster. The balloon caught fire and the Egyptians received the impression that what had been demonstrated was a machine of war for setting fire to the enemy encampments. What a pity.

Prior to Conte's pencil invention, the writing material had been nothing but a lump of pure graphite putting into a wooden stick. Instead of using the pure English graphite, Conte found a way to mix graphite in a powdered form with clay and then baked it in a way that the lead could be produced in varying degrees of hardness. Conte not only made the manageable writing material, but is also credited with inventing the machinery needed to make round lead which no other inventors who credited for pencil creation did. Up until today, Conte's brand name is still known as the pencil manufacture in France.

尼古拉斯・雅克・孔特

在這裡，我們將介紹尼古拉斯・雅克・孔特，一位來自法國的現代鉛筆發明人。出生於 1755 年，孔特不僅是一位發明家又是畫家、化學家、物理學家、工程師甚至科學家。與鉛筆的發明大不同的是，孔蒂也享有氣球戰專家的美譽，並在 1789 年與 200 位學者與科學家一同陪同拿破崙遠征埃及。不幸的是，活動在災難中結束。熱氣球起火，埃及人便認為這是一台為了火燒敵人營地而設計的戰爭機器。真是可惜。

在孔特發明鉛筆之前，書寫材料一直只是將純石墨泥投入木棍之中。代替使用純英國石墨，康特發明了一種混合石墨粉末與粘土的形式，然後經過烘烤，發展出可以製造不同硬度的鉛。康特不僅發明出容易控制的書寫材料，發明製作了圓形筆芯所需的機也歸功於他，這是其他鉛筆創造人沒做到的　。直至今日在法國，孔特的品牌名稱仍然被稱為鉛筆製造商。

必考字彙表

字彙	詞性	中譯	反義詞	中譯
Reputation	*n.*	名譽	Notoriety	惡名昭彰
Warfare	*n.*	戰爭	Peace	和平
Ensure	*v.*	保證	Deny	否認
Inclusion	*n.*	包含	Exclusion	不包含
Academic	*n.*	學者		
Accompany	*v.*	陪同	Ignore	忽略
Expedition	*n.*	遠征		
Disaster	*n.*	災害	Fortune	好運
Impression	*n.*	印象		
Demonstrate	*v.*	展示		
Encampment	*n.*	紮營		
Varying	*adj.*	不同的	Constant	一致的
Manageable	*adj.*	可控制的	Unfeasible	不可實現的
Machinery	*n.*	機械		

01
Part
飲食民生

02
Part
歷史懷舊

03
Part
現代實用科技

04
Part
資訊知識

13-2 試題演練

牛刀小試

1. It is a pity that many _____ customs got lost over time.

   A. previous   B. historical
   C. modern   D. ancient

2. It is difficult to judge a person by his _____.

   A. inside   B. exterior
   C. interior   D. core

3. The seeds contain a _____ substance that is known to kill human.

   A. toxic   B. harmless
   C. safe   D. pollution

4. Only qualified workers are allowed to use this machine because it is _____ to handle.

   A. clumsy   B. awkward
   C. handy   D. easy

5. This restaurant ruined its _____ by using expired ingredients.

   A. respect
   B. status
   C. reputation
   D. stand

6. The _____ of the parents in the discussions for the school event was a great idea.

   A. include
   B. exclude
   C. exclusion
   D. inclusion

7. Columbus had only three ships under his command on his first _____ to the New World.

   A. experience
   B. exercise
   C. expedition
   D. examination

8. Teachers have to be very flexible when working with students who have _____ needs.

   A. verying
   B. vary
   C. very
   D. varying

01 Part 飲食民生

02 Part 歷史懷舊

03 Part 現代實用科技

04 Part 資訊知識

1. **(B)** 空白處應填入形容詞，而句尾的 over time 顯示出 historical 為正確解答。

2. **(B)** 由句意可知空格處應填入「外在」A 選項 inside,B 選項 interior 和，因此答案為 exterior，表示很難以他的外表去評定一個人。

3. **(A)** 由文句可知空白處應填入「中毒」的形容詞，表示種子包含已知能殺害人類的有毒物質，故 B 選項的 harmless 和 C 選項的 safe 均不符合。D 選項為 pollution 名詞亦不符合，其中若 B 選項改為 harmful 可以選，因此答案為 toxic。

4. **(B)** 由句子開頭的「only qualified workers are allowed」可知這個機器不容易使用，所以只有 qualified workers 能操作。因此空白處應填寫 awkward。

5. **(C)** 這個空格應填入名詞，所以 a 跟 d 可以先刪除。由語句及字彙則可得知 reputation 為正確解答，表示餐廳使用過期的成分而損及自己的名聲。

6. **(D)** 由 The _____ of 的句構中得知其後應加名詞，a 和 b 為動詞故可先刪去，所以答案為 c 或 d，又由文句我們了解到 inclusion 是比較適當的答案。

7. **(C)** 由 his first _____ 的句構中得知其後應加名詞，由文句及字彙可以得知 expedition 是最好的答案。

8. **(D)** 首先，a 這個字不存在。再者 needs 之前應加形容詞，因此 varying 為正確答案，表達出不同需求，句中的意思是當與不同需求的學生共事時，老師必須非常有彈性。

Unit 14　14-1
Typewriter
打字機
by *Christopher Latham Sholes*

Typewriter　MP3 27

Many kids today might have never heard about typewriter. Not to mention have ever used one. It might be hard for some people to imagine that a typewriter was once the greatest invention of the century and was widely used by professional writers, in offices, and for business correspondence. A typewriter is a writing machine that has one character on each key press. The machine prints characters by making ink impressions in a moveable type letterpress printing.

Typewriters, like other practical products such as automobiles, telephones, and refrigerators, the invention was developed by numerous inventors. The very first record of the typewriter invention was back in 1575. In 1575, an Italian printmaker, Francesco Rampazzetto, invented the "scrittura tattile" which is a machine to impress letters in papers. Hundreds of years passed by and many different types or typewriters were being developed. However, no commercially practical machine was created. It was until 1829, an American inventor William Austin Burt patented a

Unit 14
Typewriter by Christopher Latham Sholes

01
Part
飲食民生

02
Part
歷史懷舊

03
Part
現代實用科技

04
Part
資訊知識

machine called the "Typographer" which is listed as the "first typewriter". Although, the design was still not practical enough for the market since it was slower than handwriting. In 1865, Rasmus Malling-Hansen from Denmark invented the first commercially sold typewriter, called the Hansen Writing Ball. It was successfully sold in Europe. In the US, the first commercially successful typewriter was invented by Christopher Latham Sholes in 1868.

Another 50 years later, the typewriter designs had reached a standard. Most typewriters followed the concept that each key was attached to a type bar with a corresponding letter molded. The platen was mounted on a carriage which moved left or right, automatically advancing the typing position horizontally after each character was typed. The paper rolled around the typewriter's platen. For decades, the typewriter was the major tool for work. It was until the early 1980s did typewriters start to be replaced by word processors and eventually personal computers.

Typewriter now is considered a vintage. Many companies stopped manufacturing it anymore. Therefore, if you still have one in your home, take good care of it because it might be worth a fortune in the future.

打字機

許多孩子今天可能未曾聽過打字機，更別說是曾經使用過打字機。有人可能很難想像，打字機曾經是本世紀最偉大的發明，廣泛使用於專業作家，在辦公室裡以及利用於商業信函。打字機是一個寫作的機器，一個按鍵一個字母。機器利用活字凸版印刷通過墨水打印字符。

打字機，如同其他實用的產品，如汽車、電話和冰箱，是由眾多的發明人所開發出來的。打字機發明的第一個記錄最早在 1575 年。1575 年，意大利的版畫家，弗朗西斯，發明了「scrittura tattile」，這是一台用來打字的機器。幾百年過去了，很多不同類型的打字機被開發出來。然而，沒有商業實用機的創建。直到 1829 年，美國發明家威廉·奧斯汀伯特申請了一台機器的專利稱為「字體設計」，它被列為「第一台打字機」。雖然，設計仍然不夠實用，因為它比寫字要緩慢。1865 年，來自丹麥的拉斯穆斯莫林-漢森發明了第一台在市場上銷售的打字機，叫做漢森寫作球。它成功地在歐洲銷售。在美國，第一個商業成功的打字機是在 1868 年由克里斯托弗·萊瑟姆·肖爾斯所發明的。

50 年後，打字機的設計已經達到了標準。大多數打字機都是以每個鍵被附加到與相應的字母模型的概念。壓板被安裝在一個左右滑動的滑架，自動推進每個字母，再輸入水平的打字位置。紙張是圍繞在打字機的滾筒上。幾十年來，打字機是工作的主要工具。直到 1980 年代初期，打字機開始由文字處理器和個人電腦取代。

打字機，現在被認為是一個古董。很多公司停止製造它了。因此，如果你仍然有一台在你家，請照顧好它，因為它可能未來會非常值錢。

必考字彙表

字彙	詞性	中譯	反義詞	中譯
Widely	*adv.*	廣泛地	Narrowly	狹窄地
Correspondence	*n.*	一致	Difference	不同
Character	*n.*	性格		
Impression	*n.*	印象		
Movable	*adj.*	可移動的	Immovable	不可移動的
Numerous	*adj.*	許多的	Miniature	小型的
Printmaker	*n.*	版畫複製家		
Handwriting	*n.*	手寫		
Reach	*v.*	達到	Inability	無能
Standard	*n.*	標準	Aberration	脫離常軌
Concept	*n.*	觀念		
Mold	*v.*	塑造		
Platen	*n.*	壓版		
Carriage	*n.*	滑動架		
Processor	*n.*	處理器		
Eventually	*adj.*	最後	Immediately	立即
Vintage	*n.*	某年代的產品		
Fortune	*n.*	財富	Poverty	貧窮

01
Part
飲食民生

02
Part
歷史懷舊

03
Part
現代實用科技

04
Part
資訊知識

Born and raised in Pennsylvania, Christopher Latham Sholes-born on February 14th, 1819, was educated to became a printer as his 3 brothers. He became an editor of the post at Madison and founded a weekly newspaper called the Southport Telegraph. Different from other newspapers, the Southport Telegraph would give free ad space to any writers or teachers who have thoughts about the society. It is because Soles believed that people should communicate as much as possible to bring together thoughts. After the Southport Telegraph, Sholes also worked or funded several different newspapers, such as Republican papers, the Milwaukee Daily Sentinel and News, even the Federal Post.

Because of his long experiences in journalism and politics, he understood the pain in long articles writing ink smug, misunderstood due to messing hand writings, etc. were all caused by hand writing. Therefore, he invented a machine that would do the task using preset type and a treadle which we called "typewriter" now. Of course there were many other people invented typing machines years before him, but his invention was different. Sholes' creation was to carve each single letter onto a short metal bar. The very first prototype was built in 1867. Later on, he and his partners worked on a simplified version in order to produce typewriters that were affordable for general public.

Another great invention that Sholes did which made him the "inventor of typewriter" was his keyboard design. The earliest typing machines usually arranged the letters in an alphabetical order. It is not hard for us to imagine that it would jam easily while typing. Sholes changed the order of the keys as he created prototype after prototype of his machine, trying to eliminate the most frequently occurring jams. The layout kept frequently combined letters separated mechanically, which limited the number of possible collisions between type bars. The keyboard he created is called the Qwerty Keyboard which is what we still use today.

Because of Sholes creation, it opened office careers to women. It was because of his typewriter, typewriter manufacturers started to train women as typists and offered both machine and operator as a package to clients. This was the beginning of women working in offices.

01
Part
飲食民生

02
Part
歷史懷舊

03
Part
現代實用科技

04
Part
資訊知識

克里斯托佛・萊瑟姆・肖爾斯

於 1819 年 2 月 14 日出生於賓州的克里斯托弗・萊瑟姆・肖爾斯與他的三個兄弟一起被教育要成為一位打印員。他成為了麥迪遜一家新聞社的編輯，並創辦了一家週報叫做南港電訊報。與其他報紙不同的是，南港電訊報每天都給予對於社會上擁有想法的作家或教師免費的（寫作）空間。這是因為肖爾斯認為，人們應該盡可能地匯集想法並溝通。南港電訊報後，肖爾斯還曾任職或資助了幾個不同的報紙，如共和黨報紙，密爾沃基哨兵日報和新聞，甚至聯邦日報。

由於他長期在新聞和政治圈的經驗，他理解寫長篇文章所造成的手痛，油墨的沾染，或因為手寫字跡所造成的誤會。因此，他發明了一種使用預置和踏板的機器，我們稱之為「打字機」。當然，還有許多其他人在肖爾斯之前發明了輸入設備，但與他的發明是不同的。肖爾斯的創作是雕刻每一個字母到一個短的金屬條。第一個原型是建於 1867 年。後來，他和他的夥伴，開始生產一般大眾可以負擔得起的簡易型打字機。

另一個肖爾斯的偉大發明使他被認定為打字機的發明家是他的鍵盤設計。最早的打字機是按字母順序排列。我們不難想像它會很容易在打字時堵塞。肖爾斯改造了鍵盤的順序。他做了非常多的樣本，企圖消除最常堵塞的按鍵，這個排列分開了經常結合的字母，限制了按鍵之間可能的碰撞次數。他創建的鍵盤被稱為 QWERTY 鍵盤，這是我們今天仍然使用的東西。

由於肖爾斯的創作，它使職業婦女進入了辦公室。因為他的打字機，使得打字機製造商開始培訓女性打字員，並提供機器和操作員作為一個整體服務給客戶。這是婦女在辦公室裡工作的開始。

字彙

字彙	詞形	中譯	反義詞	中譯
Republican	*adj.*	共和國的	Monarchist	君主主義的
Sentinel	*n.*	哨兵		
Federal	*adj.*	美國聯邦政府的		
Journalism	*n.*	新聞業		
Politics	*n.*	政治		
Misunderstand	*v.*	誤解	Understanding	了解
Task	*n.*	任務		
Treadle	*n.*	踏板		
Creation	*n.*	創造	Destruction	破壞
Carve	*v.*	雕刻		
Simplified	*v.*	精簡化	Complex	複雜的
Affordable	*adj.*	負擔得起的	Unaffordable	負擔不起的
General	*adj.*	一般的	Specific	特殊的
Arrange	*v.*	安排	Disarrange	使混亂
Alphabetical	*adj.*	按字母次序的		
Eliminate	*v.*	排除	Retain	保留
frequently	*adv.*	頻繁地	Rarely	難得地
Collision	*n.*	碰撞	Avoidance	避開

14-2 試題演練

牛刀小試

1. People are upset because the decrease in crude oil price hasn't resulted in a _____ drop in gasoline price.

   A. together   B. simultaneously
   C. correspondence   D. corresponding

2. After _____ consultations with the school advisor, she decided to become a business major.

   A. number   B. some
   C. numerous   D. couple

3. The _____ of living in this country has certainly risen over the last few years.

   A. qualify   B. class
   C. level   D. standard

4. It is hard for any parent to accept that _____ a baby will grow up, and move away from home.

   A. even   B. later
   C. maybe   D. eventually

5. The famous writer, Geoffrey Ward, once said that _____ is merely history's first draft.

   A. journal

   B. critic

   C. journalism

   D. criticism

6. The whale is the largest mammal in _____.

   A. planet

   B. creation

   C. history

   D. country

7. The biggest challenge for the new government is to do something to create more _____ housing for lower income families.

   A. afford

   B. cheaper

   C. costly

   D. affordable

8. It is very rare to have 2 airplanes to have a mid-air _____.

   A. break

   B. collision

   C. pass by

   D. accident

01 Part 飲食民生

02 Part 歷史懷舊

03 Part 現代實用科技

04 Part 資訊知識

1. (D) 空白應填入形容詞，因此解答為 corresponding。表示人們感到苦惱因為原油的油價下降並未造成相對應的汽油油價的下跌。

2. (C) 空白應填入形容詞，因此解答為 numerous。表示在與學校諮詢人員數次的洽談後，她決定要成為商業主修。

3. (D) Standard of living 是非常常用的語句，因此答案為 standard。

4. (B) 由文句及字彙可知 eventually 是最適合的解答。表示對父母來說，嬰兒最終會長大且離開家裡。

5. (C) 依句意，xx 學是解答，又由翻譯可看出 journalism 是比較合適的答案。

6. (B) 從選項來看，in 後面只能接 creation，因此解答為 creation。

7. (D) 空格應填入形容詞，空格前又接了 more，因此不能選 cheaper。而前面提到 The biggest challenge for the new government …以及後句的 for lower income families 都表達出是要提供一個 affordable 的居住環境， Affordable 即為正確解答。

8. **(B)** 此句句尾需用名詞，而 collision 最適合句意，因此解答為
collision。

01
Part
飲食民生

02
Part
歷史懷舊

03
Part
現代實用科技

04
Part
資訊知識

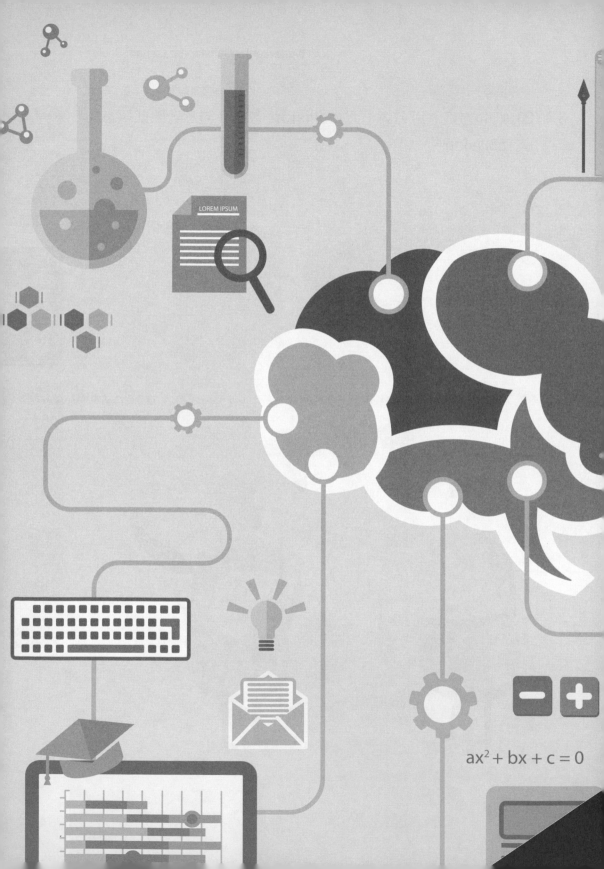

LOREM IPSUM

$$ax^2 + bx + c = 0$$

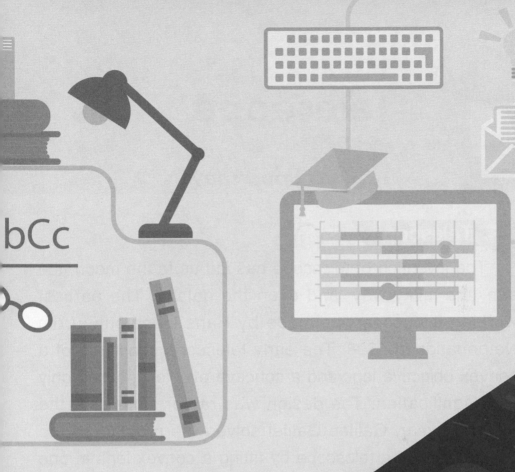

Part 3
現代實用科技

Unit 15　15-1
Telescope
望遠鏡
by *Hans Lippershey*

Telescope  MP3 29

The invention of telescope has led us to the moon, the sun, the milky way, and even the galaxy. The earliest working telescope was made by Hans Lippershey from Netherlands in 1608. The early telescope consisted of a convex objective lens and a concave eyepiece. It had only 3x magnification. The design was rather simple. In the following year, Galileo Galilei solved the problem of the construction of a telescope by fitting a convex lens in one extremity of a leaded tube and a concave lens in another one.

Galileo then improved the telescope and greatly increased the power of the telescope. His first design magnified three diameters. The second design magnified to eight diameters and then even thirty-three diameters. Because of this design, the satellites of Jupiter were discovered in 1610. Later on, the spots of sun, the phases of Venus were all found. Because of his telescope, Galileo was able to demonstrate the revolution of the satellites of Jupiter around the planet and gave predictions of the configuration. He was also able to prove the rotation of the Sun on its axis.

In 1655, Christian Huygens created the first powerful telescope of Keplerian construction. Huygens discovered the brightest of Saturn's satellites -Titan- in 1655. Four years later, he published the "Systema Saturnium", which was the first time a given true explanation of Saturn's ring- founded on observations made with the same instrument.

01
Part
飲食民生

02
Part
歷史懷舊

03
Part
現代實用科技

04
Part
資訊知識

望遠鏡

　　望遠鏡的發明帶領我們到月亮、太陽、銀河系、甚至星系。最早的望遠鏡是由來自荷蘭的漢斯・利普斯在 1608 年所發明。早期的望遠鏡包括一個凸物鏡和一個凹透鏡。它只有 3 倍的放大倍率。設計相當簡單。在第二年，伽利略在含鉛管的一個末端配裝一個凹透鏡，並在另一端裝配凸透鏡，解決了望遠鏡的結構問題。

　　伽利略之後提升了望遠鏡的結構並大大提高望遠鏡的功率。他的第一個設計放大了三個直徑。第二個設計放大了八直徑，然後是三十三直徑。由於這種設計，木星衛星於 1610 年被發現，後來，太陽的斑點及金星的軌跡皆被發現。由於他的望遠鏡，伽利略能夠示範操作木星的行星環繞軌跡，並預測衛星的結構。他還能夠證明太陽的旋轉在它的軸上。

1655 年，克里斯蒂安・惠更斯創造了開普勒建設的第一個強大的望遠鏡。惠更斯並發現了最明亮的土星衛星-Titan。4 年後，他出版了「Systema Saturnium」，這是第一次給土星環的一個真正解釋。這也是用同一台儀器觀測到的。

必考字彙表

字彙	詞形	中譯	反義詞	中譯
Consist	v.	組成		
Convex	v.	凸面的	Concave	凹面的
Magnification	n.	放大		
Construction	n.	建造	Destruction	破壞
Extremity	n.	末端	Center	中央
Diameter	n.	倍數		
Satellite	n.	衛星		
Jupiter	n.	木星		
Phase	n.	方面	Whole	全方位
Demonstrate	v.	示範操作	Conceal	隱瞞
Planet	n.	行星		
Prediction	n.	預言	Proof	證明
Configuration	n.	結構	disarrangement	擾亂
Rotation	n.	循環	Stagnation	停滯
Axis	n.	光軸		
Observation	n.	觀察	Neglect	忽視

Hans Lippershey MP3 30

Hans Lippershey, a master lens grinder and spectacle maker was born in Wesel Germany in 1570. He then got married and settled in Middelburg in Netherlands in 1594. Eight years later, he immigrated in Netherlands.

Lippershey filed a patent for telescope in 1607 and this was known as the earliest written record of a refracting telescope. There are several different versions of how Lippershey came up with the invention of the telescope. The most interesting one has to be the one that Lippershey observed two kids playing with lenses and commenting how they could make a far away weather-vane seem closer when looking at it through two lenses. Lippershey's original instrument consisted of either two convex lenses for an inverted image or a convex objective and a concave eyepiece lens so it would have an upright image.

Lippershey remained in Middelburg until he passed away in 1619.

漢斯・利普斯

身為一位鏡片研磨師和眼鏡製造商的漢斯・利普斯在 **1570** 年誕生

Part 01 飲食民生

Part 02 歷史懷舊

Part 03 現代實用科技

Part 04 資訊知識

於德國韋塞爾。爾後，在 1594 年定居於荷蘭米德爾堡，並在同一年結婚。8 年後移民荷蘭。

利普斯在 1607 年申請了望遠鏡的專利，這被稱為是折射望遠鏡最早的文字記錄。對於利普斯如何想出望遠鏡的原因有幾種不同的版本。最有趣的版本是有一次利普斯觀察到兩個小孩玩耍時的對話，他們在評論如何利用鏡頭讓一個遙遠的天氣風向標看起來似乎更接近。 利普斯的原始工具包括利用兩個凸透鏡以呈現出一個倒置的圖像，或利用凸物鏡和凹透鏡的眼鏡片以呈現出一個正面的圖像。

利普斯終其一生留在米德爾，直到他在 1619 年去世。

 字彙

字彙	詞形	中譯	反義詞	中譯
Master	*n.*	師傅	Pupil	弟子
Grinder	*n.*	研磨者		
Spectacle	*n.*	眼鏡		
Immigrate	*v.*	移民		
Refract	*v.*	折射	Straighten	弄直
Observe	*v.*	觀察	Ignore	無視
Comment	*n.*	評論		
Vane	*n.*	風向標		
Invert	*v.*	轉換		
Eyepiece	*n.*	接目鏡		
Upright	*adj.*	正的		

1. The more excuses they try to give, the bigger the problem is _____.

4. The _____ for the election now shows the first female president might be born.

A. date
B. fortune teller
C. prediction
D. news

15-2 試題演練

1. The more excuses they try to use, the bigger the problem is _____.

   A. magnificent　　　　B. magnified
   C. magnification　　　D. magnifying

2. Nurses need to be extra patient when most patients are in _____ of pain.

   A. lot　　　　　　　　B. extreme
   C. much　　　　　　　D. extremity

3. Teenagers often go through a _____ in which they don't want to be seen in public with their parents.

   A. period　　　　　　B. time
   C. phase　　　　　　 D. timing

4. The _____ for the election now shows the first female president might be born.

   A. data　　　　　　　B. fortune teller
   C. prediction　　　　 D. news

5. The unstable _____ that results makes one vulnerable to a cascade of change.

   A. configuration   B. construction
   C. concentration   D. confirmation

6. She is under close _____ at the hospital after the fire incident.

   A. observed   B. observable
   C. observing   D. observation

7. People who _____ to another country often need years to get use to the new life styles.

   A. immigration   B. emigrate
   C. emigration   D. immigrate

8. In English grammar, if you _____ the subject and the verb, it often becomes a question form.

   A. convert   B. invert
   C. replace   D. rewrite

01
Part
飲食民生

02
Part
歷史懷舊

03
Part
現代實用科技

04
Part
資訊知識

1. (A) 空白處應填入與 bigger 相對應的形容詞，因此 magnificent
為正確解答。

2. (D) 乍看之下，空白應填入形容詞，但空白後面加的是 of pain 故
應填入名詞，A 選項 lot, B 選項 extreme 和 C 選項 much
均不符合，所以 extremity 才是正確答案表示當大多數病患示
極度痛苦時，護士必須額外的有耐心。

3. (C) 由文句及字彙可知 phase 為正確答案。若句子改為 there is
a period of time teenagers exhibit a rebellious
behavior⋯.則可選 period。

4. (C) 由句尾的 might be born 可知這是個預測，因此答案為
prediction 表示選舉的預測顯示第一位女總統可能誕生。

5. (A) 由句意可知 configuration 是最適合的答案，其中 B 選項
construction 建築，C 選項 concentration 集中和 D 選項
confirmation 確認均不符合。

6. (D) 動詞之後應接名詞，因此 observation 為正確答案。另一個
常見的考法為⋯under⋯scrutiny⋯在⋯之下受到檢視。

7. **(D)** 此題為區分 emigrate 和 immigrate 的用法，空格處填入動詞，又因是「移民到」一個國家，因此正確答案為 immigrate。其中 immigrate 為子句中的動詞，而本句中主要動詞是 need。須特別注意。

8. **(B)** 空格應填入「交換」一詞，因此正確答案為 invert 表示在英語語法中，如果你將主詞和動詞至換，通常成了問題的形式了。

01
Part
飲食民生

02
Part
歷史懷舊

03
Part
現代實用科技

04
Part
資訊知識

Unit 16　16-1
Airplane
飛機
by *The Wright Brothers*

Airplane MP3 31

According to the document from IATA in 2011, 2.8 billion passengers were carried by airplane, which means in average there are 690,000 passengers in the air at any given moment. Air travel is known as the safest way to travel and it shortens the distance between countries. How would the world be today without the invention of airplane? We would never know.

The first airplane was invented by Orville and Wilbur Wright in 1903. Before the Wright's invention, many people made numerous attempts to fly like birds. In 1799, Sir George Cayley designed the first fixed-wing aircraft. In 1874, Felix duTemple made the first attempt at powered flight by hopping off the end of a ramp in a steam-driven monoplane. In 1894, the first controlled flight was made by Otto Lilienthal by shifting his body weight. Inspired by Lilienthal, the Wright brothers experimented with aerodynamic surfaces to control an airplane in flight and later on made the first airplane that was powered and controllable.

The first aircraft soared to an altitude of 10 feet, traveled 120 feet, and landed 12 seconds after takeoff. The miracle 12 seconds led to the invention of jets which are now being used for military and commercial airlines, even space flights. The jet engine was developed by Frank Whittle of the United Kingdom and Hans von Ohain of Germany in late 1930s. Because jet engine can fly much faster and at higher altitudes, it made all the international flights possible these days.

01
Part
飲食民生

02
Part
歷史懷舊

03
Part
現代實用科技

04
Part
資訊知識

飛機

據國際航空運輸協會在 2011 年的文件指出，一年中一共有 28 億的乘客搭乘飛機，這意味著無論任何時候都有平均 69 萬位乘客在空中飛行。航空旅行號稱是最安全的旅行方式，它縮短了國與國之間的距離。如果沒有飛機的發明，今天這個世界會變如何？我們永遠不會知道。

在奧維爾和威爾，萊特於 1903 年發明第一架飛機以前，很多人嘗試了像鳥一樣的飛翔方式。 1799 年，喬治・凱利爵士設計了第一架固定翼的飛機。 1874 年，菲利克斯・杜湯普跳躍過斜坡，利用蒸汽驅動單翼，第一次嘗試動力飛行。 1894 年，奧托・李林塔爾利用轉移他的體重，創造出第一架可控飛行機。由於李林塔爾的啟發，萊特兄弟實驗氣動表面來控制飛行的飛機，後來提出電動並可控制的第一架飛機。

第一架飛機飆升至 10 英尺的高空，前進 120 英尺，並在起飛後 12 秒降落。這奇蹟的 12 秒引導了噴射機的發明，目前已被用於軍事和商業航空公司，甚至太空飛行。噴射機是由英國的法蘭克·惠特爾和德國的漢斯·馮歐韓在 1930 年代後期所開發。由於噴射機能飛得更快，更高，這讓所有的國際航班成為可能。

必考字彙表

字彙	詞形	中譯	反義詞	中譯
Average	*n.*	平均	Extreme	極端
Shorten	*v.*	縮短	Lengthen	使加長
Numerous	*adj.*	許多的	Few	少許的
Attempt	*v.*	試圖	Retreat	撤退
Hop	*v.*	跳躍		
Ramp	*n.*	斜坡		
Monoplane	*n.*	單翼機		
Shift	*v.*	轉移		
Inspire	*v.*	驅使	Depress	使沮喪
Experiment	*n.*	實驗		
Aerodynamic	*adj.*	航空動力學的		
Surface	*n.*	表面	Inner	內部的
Soar	*v.*	飛騰	Plummet	落下
Altitude	*n.*	高度	Nadir	最低點
Miracle	*n.*	奇蹟	Expectation	預期

The Wright Brothers

The Wright brothers, Orville (August 19, 1871-January 30, 1948) and Wilbur (April 16, 1867-May 30, 1912), were two American brothers, born and raised with 6 brothers and sisters in a small town in Ohio. Even though Orville and Wilbur were 4 years apart, they shared same interests and had very similar life experiences.

When both of them were kids in 1878, their father bought them a toy "helicopter" which was a toy version of an invention of French aeronautical pioneer Alphose Penaud. This device was the initial spark of the brother's interest in flying. Both brothers attended high school but neither of them got a diploma. Orville started a printing business in 1889 which Wilbur later on joined. Three years later, the brothers opened a bicycle repair and sales shop, and in 1896 they started to manufacture their own brand. Even though they were running the bicycle business, they still held their interests in flying. Therefore, when they found out information about the dramatic glides by Otto Lilienthal in Germany, they decided to use the endeavor to fund their interest in flight.

In designing their airplane, the Wrights drew upon a number of bicycle concepts such as the importance of balance and control, the strong but lightweight structures, the concerns about wind resistance and aerodynamic shape of the operator. To them, flying is just like riding a bicycle. Together, the Wright brothers developed the first successful airplane in Kitty Hawk, North Carolina in 1903. They became national heroes. Named as the fathers of modern aviation, they developed innovative technology and inspired imaginations around the world.

萊特兄弟

　　萊特兄弟，奧維爾（1871 年 8 月 19 日－1948 年 1 月 30 日）和威爾伯（1867 年 4 月 16 日－5 月 30 日，1912 年），是兩個美國兄弟，在俄亥俄州的一個小鎮出生。與 6 個兄弟姐妹一起長大，即使奧維爾和威爾伯相差 4 歲，他們分享相同的興趣並有著非常相似的人生經歷。

　　1878 年當他們倆都還是小孩時，他們的父親送了他們一個「直升機」玩具，這是法國航空先驅 Alphose Penaud 一項發明的玩具版本。該裝置正是燃起兄弟倆對飛行產生興趣的火花。兩兄弟都唸了高中，但都沒有拿到文憑。奧維爾在 1889 年開始了印刷業務，威爾伯則後來加入。 3 年後，兄弟倆開了一家自行車修理和銷售的店。在 1896 年，他們開始生產自己的品牌。即使他們正在運行自行車業務，他們仍然堅持自己對飛行的興趣。因此，當他們發現了德國奧托・里鄰塔爾戲劇性的滑軌信息，他們決定用他們的努力來資助他們對飛行的興趣。

在設計飛機時，萊特兄弟利用了許多自行車概念，如平衡和控制，堅固但重量輕的結構，風的阻力和操作氣動時外形的重要性等。對他們來說，飛行就像騎自行車。兄弟倆一起在 1903 年北卡羅來納州研製了第一架飛機。他們成為了國家英雄。並被命名為現代航空之父。他們研發出創新的技術並激發了世界各地的想像力。

字彙

字彙	詞形	中譯	反義詞	中譯
Experience	*n.*	經驗	Inexperience	無經驗
Helicopter	*n.*	直升機		
Aeronautical	*adj.*	航空的	Ground	地面的
Pioneer	*n.*	開拓者	Cease	終止
Initial	*adj.*	開始	Final	最後
Attend	*v.*	出席	Absent	缺席
Diploma	*n.*	文憑		
Repair	*v.*	修理	Damage	破壞
Dramatic	*adj.*	戲劇化的	Natural	自然的
Glide	*v.*	滑行	Walk	行走
Endeavor	*v.*	努力	Passive	消極
Structure	*n.*	構造		
Resistance	*n.*	阻力	Acceptance	接受
Aviation	*n.*	航空		

01
Part
飲食民生

02
Part
歷史懷舊

03
Part
現代實用科技

04
Part
資訊知識

牛刀小試

1. In Greek mythology, the species became associated with _____ gods.

    A. numerous　　　　B. number

    C. several　　　　　D. a few

2. With fewer than 10,000 fighters, the army was forced to _____.

    A. stand by　　　　B. push further

    C. retreat　　　　　D. attempt

3. John Kennedy's hard work _____him to become a politician.

    A. inspiration　　　B. enforced

    C. inspired　　　　　D. encouraged

4. The temperature will _____ to around 5℃ on Monday due to the cold air mass.

    A. pump　　　　　　B. plummet

    C. decent　　　　　D. depress

5. The captain always announces the ground _____ after take off.

    A. height   B. speed

    C. temperature   D. altitude

6. Only qualified personals have the access to the tarmac side of the airports and the _____ facilities.

    A. airplane   B. air force

    C. Aerodynamic   D. Aeronautical

7. Her _____ reaction after hearing someone shout "Danger" was to crawl under the table.

    A. initial   B. instantly

    C. initially   D. immediately

8. Infants catch colds easily because their _____ is low.

    A. body   B. resistance

    C. acceptance   D. hostility

01 Part 飲食民生

02 Part 歷史懷舊

03 Part 現代實用科技

04 Part 資訊知識

題目解析

1. **(A)** 空格處應該填入形容詞，由文句及字會可以挑選出 numerous 是最適當的答案。

2. **(C)** 由文句一開頭的 fewer 可以理解軍隊是被迫撤退，因此答案為 retreat。

3. **(C)** 空格處應填入動詞，因此 a 可以先刪除，而由字意可以選出 inspired 為正確解答。由 hard work 這項特質得知，是由 hard work 去 inspire 他成為政客，故句意為 inspire or motivate 人。而 encourage 比較是 A encourage B 去做某事。

4. **(B)** 由於是用於溫度下降的動詞，因此解答為 plummet。

5. **(D)** 在飛機上，機長通常會說明對地面的高度，而此時會使用 altitude，而不是 height。

6. **(D)** 空格需填入形容詞，因此答案為 c 或 d。而 c 是航空動力學的意思，因此答案為 aeronautical。

7. **(A)** 依照文法，空格需填入形容詞，其於選項均為 adv，因此可以簡單的選出答案為 initial。

8. **(B)** 由文句及字詞可以挑選出 resistance 是最適合的答案。表示
嬰兒很容易感冒因為他們的抵抗力弱。

01
Part
飲食民生

02
Part
歷史懷舊

03
Part
現代實用科技

04
Part
資訊知識

Unit 17　17-1
Automobile
汽車
by *Karl Benz*

Automobile　MP3 33

There were many people who made a great contribution to the invention of different types of automobiles. But it was until Karl Benz built the first petrol automobile, did vehicles become practical and went into actual production.

The first gasoline-powered automobile built by Karl Benz contained an internal combustion engine. He built it in 1885 in Mannheim and was granted a patent for his automobile in 1886. Two years later, he began the first production of automobiles. In 1889, Gottlied Daimler and Wilhelm Maybach also designed a vehicle from scratch in Stuttgart. In 1895, a British engineer, Frederick William Lanchester built the first four-wheeled petrol driven automobile and also patented the disc brake. In between 1895 and 1898, the first electric starter was installed on the Benz Velo.

By the 1930s, most of the mechanical technology used in today's automobiles had been invented. But due to the Great Depression, the number of auto manufacturers declined sharply. Many companies consolidated and matured. After that, the automobile market was booming for decades until the 1970s. The 1970s were turbulent years for automakers. Starting from the 1973 oil crisis, stricter automobile emissions control and safety requirements, the market was no longer dominated by the US makers. Japan became the world's leader of car production for a while. Until 2009, China took over the leading position and became the world's leading car manufacturer with production greater than all other countries.

汽車

　　許多人都曾對發明不同類型的汽車有偉大的貢獻，但直到卡爾‧賓士製造了第一台汽油汽車，汽車才真正能被有效利用，走進實際生產。

　　卡爾‧賓士製作了第一個汽油動力汽車內所用的內燃機。他於 1885 年製作，並在 1886 年於曼海姆取得第一台汽車的專利。2 年後他開始了第一輛汽車的生產。1889 年，古特蘭‧戴姆勒和威廉‧邁巴赫也在斯圖加特開始了汽車的設計。1895 年，一名英國工程師，腓特烈‧威廉在曼徹斯特製造了第一台四輪驅動的汽油汽車，並申請了盤式制動器的專利。在 1895 年和 1898 年間，賓士在車內安裝了首款的電動起動器。

　　到了 1930 年代，今天汽車內使用的大部分機械技術已被發明出來。但由於經濟大蕭條，汽車製造業的數量急劇下降。許多公司合併且趨於成熟。在此之後，汽車市場蓬勃發展了幾十年直到 70 年代。70 年代是汽車製造商的動盪年代。從 1973 年的石油危機到更嚴格的汽車排放控制和安全的要求，市場不再由美國製造商主導地位。有段時間日本成為世界汽車生產的龍頭。直到 2009 年，中國接手領先地位，並成為全球領先的汽車製造商，生產量超過所有其他國家。

必考字彙表

字彙	詞形	中譯	反義詞	中譯
Practical	*adj.*	實用的	Impractical	不切實際的
Contain	*v.*	包含	Exclude	排除在外
Combustion	*n.*	燃燒	Calm	鎮定下來
Grant	*v.*	給予	Prohibit	禁止
Depression	*n.*	蕭條	Happiness	快樂
Consolidate	*v.*	合併	Split up	分開
Mature	*adj.*	成熟的	Undeveloped	未開發的
Turbulent	*adj.*	騷動的	Orderly	有秩序的
Crisis	*n.*	危機	Breakthrough	突破性的進展
Dominate	*v.*	統治	Obey	聽從

Karl Benz MP3 34

Most of the time, when people hear the name Karl Benz, they automatically associate the term with the luxury car brand. But not everyone knows that the world's first practical gasoline powered vehicle was actually invented by him.

Karl Friedrich Benz was born in Muhlburg, Germany on November 25th, 1844. Because of his mother's persistence, Benz attended the local Grammar School in Harlsruhe and was a prodigious student. Benz was very smart. At the age of 15, he already followed his father's steps toward locomotive engineering, and passed the entrance exam for mechanical engineering at University of Karlsruhe. After graduation, Benz did some professional training in several different companies, but he didn't feel like he fit in any of them. So at the age of 27, he launched the Iron Foundry and Mechanical Workshop in Mannheim with August Ritter. Business didn't go well though. Benz eventually bought out Ritter's share and started his development of new engines. He created the very first two-stroke engine in 1878, and was granted a patent for in 1879. He then patented the speed regulation system, the ignition using sparks with battery, the gear shift, the water radiator, and many other automobile parts.

It was 1885 that Benz finished his creation for the first gasoline powered automobile which he named Motorwagen. It featured wire wheels with a four-stroke engine and a very advanced coil ignition. It also had the evaporative cooling system. The Motorwagen was patented on January 29,

01
Part
飲食民生

02
Part
歷史懷舊

03
Part
現代實用科技

04
Part
資訊知識

1886. The following year, Benz created the 2nd generation of the Motorwagen. Benz started to sell the Motorwagen in 1888, which is the first commercially available automobile in history. The brand Benz became famous since then. Benz retired from design management in 1903 but remained as director on the Board of Management. He passed away at the age of 84. The Benz home now has been designated as historic and is used as a scientific meeting facility.

卡爾・賓士

　　大多數時候，當人們聽到賓士這個名字，他們通常會自動與豪華汽車品牌連接。但並不是每個人都知道，世界上第一台實用的汽油動力車實際上就是由他發明的。

　　卡爾・弗里德里希・賓士於 1844 年 11 月 25 日誕生於德國的穆伯格。由於他母親的堅持，賓士參加了邢蘇赫當地的文法學校，且是一個驚人的學生。賓士非常的聰明。在 15 歲的時候，他已經跟隨父親的腳步走向汽車工程，並通過卡爾斯魯厄大學機械工程的入學考試。他畢業於 1864 年。在 19 歲畢業後，賓士在幾個不同的公司做了一些專業的訓練，但他並不覺得自己適合任何一份工作。因此，在 27 歲時，他與奧格斯・里特在曼海姆開起了鋼鐵鑄造和機械的工廠。雖然，經營並不順利。賓士最終還是買下了里特的市場份額，並開始了他新的發展引擎。他於 1878 年創建的第一個二段引擎，並在 1879 年獲得了專利。他隨後申請了變速系統，利用火花與電池的點火器，排擋，水散熱器，

01
Part
飲食民生

及許多其他汽車零件的專利。

1885 年，賓士完成了他創作的第一台汽油動力汽車，他命名 Motorwagen。它擁有鋼絲輪與一個四段引擎和一個非常先進的點火線圈。它也有蒸氣冷卻系統。Motorwagen 在 1886 年 1 月 29 日獲得了發明專利，賓士並創造了第二代的 Motorwagen。賓士於 1888 年開始銷售 Motorwagen。這是歷史上的第一個商用汽車。自那時以來，該品牌賓士名聲大振。賓士在 1903 年由設計管理職務退休，但仍作為管理委員會的主任。他享年 84 歲。賓士的家目前已被指定為歷史建築，並作為一個科學會議的設施。

02
Part
歷史懷舊

03
Part
現代實用科技

04
Part
資訊知識

字彙

字彙	詞形	中譯	反義詞	中譯
Persistence	*n.*	堅持	Transience	稍縱即逝
Prodigious	*adj.*	巨大的	Small	微小的
locomotive	*adj.*	動力的		
Entrance	*n.*	入學		
Launch	*v.*	開始從事	Finish	結束
Stroke	*n.*	衝程		
Regulation	*n.*	規章	Lawlessness	無法律
Ignition	*n.*	點火開關		
Radiator	*n.*	冷卻器		
Evaporative	*adj.*	蒸發的		
Generation	*n.*	世代		
Designate	*v.*	定名為	Reject	駁回

 **牛刀小試**

1. This TV program gives a lot of _____ suggestions on how to raise a kid.

   A. practice
   B. particular
   C. practical
   D. partial

2. Gasoline which _____ lead is no longer available in most countries.

   A. consider
   B. exclude
   C. without
   D. contains

3. Gas leak is the most common spontaneous _____.

   A. combustion
   B. explode
   C. combination
   D. bursting

4. The company has _____ 2 sales departments to reduce costs.

   A. gather
   B. consolidated
   C. combination
   D. gathering

5. A _____ period of history often creates a new generation.

   A. peaceful   B. unforgettable

   C. turbulent   D. trouble

6. The _____ increase in housing prices in the bay area forces many young people to move in with their parents.

   A. slightly   B. gradually

   C. persistent   D. slowly

7. The government has a strict _____ regarding drug smuggling.

   A. punishment   B. renovation

   C. regulation   D. reservation

8. In the natural cycle, water _____ and then later falls as rain.

   A. evaporation   B. evaporative

   C. evaporates   D. evaporating

01 Part 飲食民生

02 Part 歷史懷舊

03 Part 現代實用科技

04 Part 資訊知識

1. (C) 空格應填入形容 suggestions 的形容詞，由句意我們也可選出 practical 為正確解答表示電視節目給予許多如何養育小孩的實用建議。

2. (D) 由句意及字彙我們可以簡單挑出 contains 包含為正確答案，汽油 gasoline 為不可數名詞其後加單數動詞，在 which 子句中需用單數動詞即 which contains 修飾 gasoline，而句中真正的動詞為 is，故 A 選項 consider, B 選項 exclude, C 選項 without 均不符合。

3. (A) 句尾應使用名詞，所以 b 及 d 可以先刪除。又由句意，我們可以得 combustion 為正解。

4. (B) 以文法來看，完成式 has v+ed A 選項 gather 為動詞, C 選項 combination 為名詞, D 選項 gathering 為動名詞或分詞均不符合，應此 consolidated 為正確答案。

5. (C) 此句要闡述的是「動盪不安的年代」，因此正確解答為 turbulent。

6. (C) 由後半句的 forces many young people to move in with their parents 可得知，租金並非緩慢的漲，因此答案為 persistent。表示在岸邊地區不斷上漲的房價，迫使許多年輕人搬去與父母同住。

7. (C) 由句意及字彙可以理解 regulation 是最適合的答案 A 選項 punishment, B 選項 renovation, D 選項 reservation 均不符合。表示政府對關於走私毒品有嚴格的管制。

8. (C) 空格需填入動詞，因此解答為 evaporates A 選項 evaporation 為名詞, B 選項 evaporative 為形容詞, D 選項 reservating 為動名詞或分詞均不符合。在大自然的循環中，水蒸發了然後降落成了雨。

Unit 18 18-1
Stethoscope
聽診器

by *Rene Laennec*

Stethoscope MP3 35

What if doctors still check Patients' heart sounds by putting their ears on patients' chests? I bet it wouldn't be comfortable for either doctors or patients. The stethoscope was invented by a French doctor, Rene Laennec in 1816 for exact that reason. Laennec came up with the thought of stethoscope because he was uncomfortable placing his ear on women's chests to hear heart sounds. The device he created was similar to the common ear trumpet. It was made of a wooden tube and was monaural.

It was not until 1840 a stethoscope with a flexible tube was invented. Back then, the stethoscope still had only single earpiece. In 1851, Arthur Leared, a physician from Irish first came up with a binaural stethoscope. A year later, George Camman improved the design of the instrument and it has become the standard ever since.

In the early 1960s, a Harvard Medical School professor, David Littmann, created a new lighter and improved acoustic. And almost 40 years later, the first external noise reducing stethoscope was patented by Richard Deslauriers. The medical technology keeps improving. And it was just recently an open-source 3D-printed stethoscope which was based on the Littmann Cardiology 3 stethoscope was invented by Dr. Tarek Loubani.

聽診器

如果醫生需要將自己的耳朵放在患者的胸前才能檢查患者心臟的聲音會怎麼樣？我敢打賭，無論是醫生還是患者都會感到不舒服。聽診器是在 1816 年由一個法國醫生蕊內 拉埃內克所發明，而發明的原因正是如此。拉埃內克有了聽診器的想法，正是因為要他把他的耳朵放在婦女的胸部以聽到心臟聲音是非常痛苦的。他所創造的設備是類似於常見的助聽器。設計是利用一個木管的單聲道。

直到 1840 年才有軟管的單聽筒聽診器。在 1851 年，來自愛爾蘭的醫生，阿瑟・李納德第一次設計了一個雙耳聽診器。一年後，喬治卡門進化了儀器的設計，使它成為聽診器的標準。

在 1960 年初期，哈佛大學醫學院教授，大衛・利特曼，創造了一個新的、更輕的聽筒，並改進了聲學。而近爾後 40 年，第一個外部噪聲降低聽診器的專利申由理查 達斯蘿莉所申請。由於醫療技術不斷提高。就在最近，利用立得慢心臟 3 聽診器的基礎而發明的 3D 列印聽診器也由塔里克魯邦尼博士所發明。

01
Part
飲食民生

02
Part
歷史懷舊

03
Part
現代實用科技

04
Part
資訊知識

必考字彙表

字彙	詞形	中譯	反義詞	中譯
Stethoscope	n.	聽筒		
Patient	n.	病患	Doctor	醫生
Bet	v.	打賭		
Exact	adj.	精確的	Approximate	大約的
Device	n.	設備		
Similar	adj.	類似的	Different	不同的
Trumpet	n.	喇叭		
Tube	n.	管子		
Monaural	adj.	單耳的	Binaural	兩耳的
Flexible	adj.	可彎曲的	Rigid	不易彎曲的
Earpiece	n.	耳機		
Physician	n.	醫師	Patient	病患
Binaural	adj.	兩耳的	Monaural	單耳的
Instrument	n.	儀器		
Standard	n.	標準	Abnormal	不尋常的
Acoustic	adj.	聽覺的		
External	adj.	外在的	Internal	內在的

Rene Laennec MP3 36

Rene Laennec was born February on 17th, 1781 at Quimper, France. He grew up living with his uncle Guillaime Laennec who worked as a faculty of medicine at the

01
Part
飲食民生

02
Part
歷史懷舊

03
Part
現代實用科技

04
Part
資訊知識

University of Nantes. Influenced by his uncle, that's when Rene first started his study in medicine. In 1799, he happened to have the privilege of studying under some of the most famous surgeon and expert in cardiology. It was when he was 19 that he moved to Paris and studied dissection in Guillaume Duputren's laboratory.

Graduating in medicine in 1804, Laennec became an associate at the Societe de IEcole de Medicine. He then found that tubercle lesions could be present in all organs of the body and not just lungs. By 1816, at the age of 35, he was offered the position of a physician at the Necker Hospital in Paris.

Laennec is considered to be one of the greatest doctors of all times. It was him that introduced auscultation. This method involves listening and identifying various sounds made by different body organs. Before the invention of this method, doctors needed to put ears on patients' chests to diagnose patients' problems. He felt uncomfortable especially while he was diagnosing young women. This led to the innovation of a new device called stethoscope which he initially termed as "chest examiner". With stethoscope, nowadays all doctors are able to study different sounds of heart and understand patients' condition in a much more precise way. Laennec's works were way ahead of his times and had a great impact on medical science.

蕊內・拉埃內克

蕊內・拉埃內克生於 1781 年 2 月 17 日的法國，坎佩爾。他與他在南特大學擔任教師的伯父古拉梅拉埃內克一起生活。由於他伯父的影響，拉埃內克開始了他在醫學的研究。 1799 年，他在偶然的機會下與某些最有名的外科醫生和專家學習心臟病學研究。當他 19 歲時，他移居巴黎，並在紀堯姆・都普特的實驗室研究解剖。

1804 年畢業於醫藥，拉埃內克成為 Societe de lEcole de Medicine 的一員。之後他發現了結節性病變可能存在於身體的所有器官，而不僅僅是肺部。到了 1816 年，在他 35 歲的時候，他得到了巴黎內克爾醫院醫生的位子。

拉埃內克被認為是所有時代內最偉大的醫生之一。他引進了聽診技術。這種方法涉及聽力，並確定由不同的身體器官製成各種聲音。這種方法發明之前，醫生需要把耳朵放在患者的胸前以診斷病人的問題。由其當他診斷年輕女性時，這個方法令他不舒服這促使了一個新的設備的發明，稱為聽診器。他最初稱這個儀器為「胸部測試器」。因為聽診器，現在所有的醫生都能夠學習心臟的不同的聲音，並以一個更精確的方式了解患者的病情。拉埃內克的作品於是遙遙領先了他所處的時代並對醫學有很大的影響。

字彙

字彙	詞形	中譯	反義詞	中譯
Faculty	*n.*	教職員		
Influence	*v.*	影響		
Privilege	*n.*	特權	Disadvantage	不利條件
Surgeon	*n.*	外科醫生	Patient	病患
Expert	*n.*	專家	Inexperienced	沒有經驗的
Cardiology	*n.*	心臟病學		
Dissection	*n.*	解剖學		
Associate	*n.*	合夥人	Enemy	敵人
Tubercle	*n.*	小瘤		
Lesion	*n.*	器官損害		
Consider	*v.*	考慮	Ignore	無視
Auscultation	*n.*	聽診		
Involve	*v.*	使捲入	Abandon	遺棄
Diagnose	*v.*	診斷		
Precise	*adj.*	精確的	Vague	模糊不清的

01 Part 飲食民生

02 Part 歷史懷舊

03 Part 現代實用科技

04 Part 資訊知識

1. The invention of navigation system helps find the _____ destination.

    A. exactly   B. correct

    C. finally   D. exact

2. _____ hearing aid fitting is the standard of practice.

    A. Monaural   B. Binary

    C. Single   D. Double

3. Most murderers are determined to be mentally _____.

    A. stable   B. unhealthy

    C. qualified   D. abnormal

4. It is unwise to judge people by _____.

    A. internal   B. personality

    C. externals   D. outside

5. The president is a man of _____ in one country.

   A. power   B. influence
   C. rule   D. rights

6. The _____ of a company share the profit and the responsibility together.

   A. employer   B. employees
   C. inventor   D. associates

7. He passed away due to multiple _____ caused by cancer.

   A. pain   B. lesions
   C. effects   D. lesson

8. People _____ with cancer often times need to go thru chemotherapy.

   A. sick   B. defect
   C. diminish   D. diagnosed

題目解析

1. **(D)** 空格處應填入形容詞，因此 A 和 C 選項均為副詞故可先刪除。而文句所要闡述的是「精準的」意思，因此答案為 exact，表示航空系統幫助找到確切的目的地。

2. **(A)** 助聽器以單耳為主流，因此答案為 monaural，表示單耳的聽力協助裝置是標準的慣例 B 選項 binary 二元的, C 選項 single 單一的/單身的, D 選項 double 兩倍的/雙人的均不符合。

3. **(D)** 由文句及字意可以簡單選出答案為 abnormal，A 選項 stable 穩定的，B 選項 unhealthy 不健康的，C 選項 qualified 均不符合句意，表示大多數的謀殺犯均為心智不正常的。

4. **(C)** 空格處應填入名詞，文句中又是提及複數 people，因此答案為 externals。表示由外表評斷人是不明智的 A 選項 internal 內部的/內在的，B 選項 personality 個性 D 選項 outside 外部均不符合句意。

5. **(B)** 由文句可以理解空格需填入「影響力」一詞，因此解答為 influence。

6. **(D)** 公司的利益及責任是由合夥人共同承擔，因此 associates 為正確解答。主動詞是 share，share 是複數動詞，故主詞為複數名詞，故選 associates。

7. **(B)** Lesion 是形容因疾病所造成的器官損害，b 為最符合句意的，因此 b 是正確答案。

8. **(D)** 由文句可知空格處應填寫「被診斷出」一詞，其中省略了 **(who are)**，句中真動詞為 **need**，因此答案為 diagnosed。

01
Part
飲食民生

02
Part
歷史懷舊

03
Part
現代實用科技

04
Part
資訊知識

Unit 19 19-1
Helicopter
直升機
by *Igor Sikorsky*

Peanut Butter MP3 37

Different from an airplane, a helicopter relies on rotors to take off and land vertically, to hover, and to fly forward backward and laterally. Because of its flexibility, it allows taking off and landing at limited areas. Therefore, helicopters are often used for rescues or ironically wars.

The earliest reference of vertical flight originated from bamboo copter developed in 400 B.C. The theory of the bamboo copter is to spin the stick attached to a rotor. The spinning creates lift, and the toy flies when released. This is the origin of the helicopter development which scientists all over the world spent hundreds of years developing so that we can have the helicopter today.

About a thousand years later, Leonardo da Vinci created a design that was made towards vertical flight called "aerial screw". Another 300 years later, Russian scientist Mikhail Lomonosov developed a small coaxial modeled and demonstrated it to the Russian Academy. It was another 100 years later, in 1861, the word "helicopter" was named by a French inventor, Gustave de Ponton dAmecourt, who made a small, steam powered helicopter made with aluminum. Although, this model never lifted off the ground.

Since then, the helicopter development was going on all over the world, from the United States, to England, France, Denmark and even Russia. But it was not until 1942 that a helicopter designed by Igor Sikorsky reached a full-scale production. The most common helicopter configuration had a single main rotor with anti-torque tail rotor, unlike the earlier designs that had multiple rotor.

Centuries of development later, the invention of helicopter improves the transportation of people and cargo, uses for military, construction, firefighting, research, rescue, medical transport, and many others. The contributions of the helicopter are uncountable.

直升機

　與飛機不同，直升機依靠螺旋槳起飛，垂直降落，懸停，前進後退和橫向飛行。由於它的靈活性，它允許在有限的區域內起飛和降落。因此，直升機常常被用於救援或很諷刺的被用在戰爭裡。

　信不信由你，我們大家都非常熟悉的垂直飛行最早的參考，就是竹蜻蜓。這是在公元 400 年前就開發出來，我們都玩過的玩具。竹蜻蜓的理論是旋轉黏在螺旋槳上的竹籤。因為旋轉造成懸浮力，因此玩具在被釋放時會飛起。這是直升機開發的起源，科學家在世界各地花了幾百年開發，以至於我們能擁有今天的直升機。

大約一千年以後，達芬奇創造了一個垂直飛行的設計，稱為空中螺絲。300 年後，俄羅斯科學家米哈伊爾·羅蒙諾索夫開發了一個小型的同軸建模並在俄羅斯科學院展示。再 100 年後，於 1861 年，法國發明家，古斯塔夫·德龐頓做了一個小型蒸汽動力的鋁製直升機，他也是第一個命名「直升機」的人。雖然如此，這個模型卻永遠無法離開地面。此後，直升機在世界各地不停的發展，有來自美國、英國、法國、丹麥，甚至俄羅斯。直到 1942 年由伊戈爾·西科斯基設計的直升機才達到全面性的生產。最常見的直升機配置有具有抗扭矩尾槳和單一主螺旋槳。不同於早期的設計，有多個螺旋槳。

幾個世紀的發展之後，直升機的發明提高了人員和貨物的運輸，使用於軍事、建築、消防、科研、救護，醫療轉運，和許多其他地方。直升機的貢獻是不可數計的。

必考字彙表

字彙	詞形	中譯	反義詞	中譯
Helicopter	*n.*	直升機		
Rotor	*n.*	旋轉翼		
Vertically	*adv.*	垂直地	Horizontal	水平的

Hover	*v.*	停留在空中	Descend	下降
Laterally	*adv.*	橫向地		
Flexibility	*n.*	靈活性	Rigidity	死板
Rescue	*v.*	救援	Peril	危險
Ironically	*adv.*	諷刺地		
Theory	*n.*	理論		
Spin	*v.*	旋轉	Immobility	靜止
Release	*v.*	釋放	Confine	限制
Aerial	*adj.*	航空的	Terrestrial	陸地的
Coaxial	*adj.*	同軸的		
Lift	*v.*	升起		
Full-scale	*adj.*	照原尺寸的	Partial	局部的
Torque	*v.*	轉距	Stagnation	停滯

Igor Sikorsky MP3 38

Some people might recognize the name of Igor Ivanovich Sikorsky from the public airport in Fairfield County, Connecticut. No doubt that due to the great contributions from Sikorsky to the aviation industry, the airport of his hometown decided to name after him.

Sikorsky was born in Kiev, Russian Empire, on May 25th, 1889. In 1900, he went to Germany with his father who was a physics, and became interested in natural sciences. He began to experiment with flying machines and made a small rubber band powered helicopter at the age of 12. At the age of 14, he joined the Saint Petersburg Imperial Russian Naval Academy but resigned in a few years because he decided to study in Engineering instead. In 1908, he learned about the Wright brother's Flyer and Ferdinand von Zeppelin's dirigible, he immediately decided to study aviation and concentrate on aviation research for his entire life. A year later, he enrolled in ETACA engineering school in Paris to study aeronautics. At that time, Paris was the center of the aviation world.

From 1909 to 1942, Sikorsky designed or helped design at least 11 different kinds of aircrafts. Sikorsky immigrated to the United States in 1919 and founded his first company "the Sikorsky Aircraft Corporation" in 1923. In 1930, he developed the first of Pan American Airways' ocean-conquering flying boats. And in 1939, he designed the first viable helicopter named VS-300. The prototype worked fine but was not suitable for mass production. Therefore, Sikorsky used 3 years to do the modification and created the Sikorsky R-4, which became the world's first mass-produced helicopter.

Sikorsky passed away in 1972 at his hometown Connecticut.

伊戈爾・西科斯基

有些人可能會從康乃狄克州費爾菲爾德縣的大眾機場那裡認出「伊戈爾・伊万諾維奇・西科斯基」這個名字。毫無疑問的，由於西科斯基對航空業的巨大貢獻，家鄉的機場決定以他的名字來命名。

西科斯基在 1889 年 5 月 25 日，出生於俄羅斯的基輔。在 1900 年，他與擔任物理學家的父親以起前往德國，並開始對自然科學產生極大的興趣。在 12 歲時，他便開始試驗飛行器，並做了一個小型的橡皮筋動力直升機。在 14 歲時，他加入了俄羅斯聖彼得海軍學院，但在短短幾年內就休學，因為他決定專攻電機。而在 1908 年時，他得知萊特兄弟和斐迪南・馮・齊柏林的飛船，他立即決定學習航空。專注於航空研究成為了他生活的一切。一年後，他就到巴黎專攻航空學，就讀於 ETACA 工程學。當時，巴黎是世界的航空中心。

1909 年至 1942 年，西科斯基設計或幫忙設計了至少 11 個不同類型的飛機。西科斯基於 1919 年移民美國，並在 1923 年創辦了他的第一家公司「西科斯基飛機公司」。1930 年，他研製出第一台泛美航空公司的海洋征服飛行船。而在 1939 年，他設計的第一個可用的直升機，命名為 VS-300。原型做得很好，但不適合大規模生產。因此，西科斯基用了 3 年的時間做了修改和創作西科斯基 R-4，從而成為世界上第一個大規模生產的直升機。

西科斯基在 1972 年逝世於他的家鄉康乃狄克州。

01
Part
飲食民生

02
Part
歷史懷舊

03
Part
現代實用科技

04
Part
資訊知識

字彙

字彙	詞形	中譯	反義詞	中譯
Recognize	*v.*	認出	Deny	否認
Aviation	*n.*	航空		
Experiment	*n.*	實驗	Abstention	戒絕
Rubber	*n.*	橡皮		
Resign	*v.*	辭去	Sign on	簽到
Dirigible	*adj.*	可駕駛的		
Enroll	*v.*	入學	Expel	開除
Engineering	*n.*	工程學		
Aeronautics	*n.*	航空學		
Aircraft	*n.*	飛機		
Conquer	*v.*	克服	Surrender	放棄
Viable	*adj.*	可實行的	Unpractical	不切實際的
Suitable	*adj.*	適合的	Inappropriate	不適當的
Modification	*n.*	修改		

01
Part
飲食民生

02
Part
歷史懷舊

03
Part
現代實用科技

04
Part
資訊知識

19-2 試題演練

牛刀小試

1. The French flag has three _____ stripes in white, blue and red.

   A. horizontal
   C. narrow

   B. oversized
   D. vertical

2. As a working mother, she needs to find a job with _____ hours in order to take care of her kids.

   A. fixed
   C. flexible

   B. shorten
   D. unusual

3. _____, she rejected the job offer that everyone wanted.

   A. Unfortunately
   C. Luckily

   B. Ironically
   D. Interesting

4. Breaking News-A baby monkey was captured in the city, and later _____ in the forest.

   A. released
   C. bring

   B. reborn
   D. raise

5. Many cosmetic companies now support no scientific ____ on animals.

    A. test   B. expert

    C. experiment   D. experimentation

6. She _____ from her position after knowing she is pregnant.

    A. stop   B. quit

    C. resigned   D. dropped

7. It takes a lot of courage to _____ your fear.

    A. facing   B. brave

    C. conquer   D. ignore

8. Many people prefer to _____ the car engine in order to increase the horse power.

    A. modification   B. modify

    C. magnify   D. magnification

題目解析

1. (D) 空白處應填入「垂直的」，所以解答為 vertical，表示法國國旗須有 3 個條紋白、藍和紅。

2. (C) 由句意及字彙我們可以挑選出 flexible 為最適合的選項。

3. (B) 句首應使用副詞做為強調，因此 d 可以先刪除。而由句意來看，ironically 是最好的答案。

4. (A) 此句為過去式，因此選項為 a 或 b，而由句意來看只有 released 為過去式動詞，故其為正確答案。

5. (D) 空白應填入名詞，又由語句裡可得知 experimentation 是正確答案。

6. (C) 辭去工作，一般使用「resign from」，因此 c 為正確答案。表示在得知她懷孕時，她辭職了。

7. (C) 由字意來看，空格應填入「面對」或「克服」一詞，但選項中的 facing 在文法上是錯誤的，因此正確答案為 conquer。

8. (B) 空白應填入動詞，因此可以先刪除 a 和 c。由句意和詞彙我們又可挑出 modify 為正確答案。表示許多人寧願修改車引擎以增加馬力。

Unit 20 20-1
Dynamite
火藥
by *Alfred Nobel*

 **Dynamite** MP3 39

Dynamite came from the Greek word 'Dynamis' which means "Power".

The 18th and the 19th centuries are known as the boom-years of the industrial revolution for the western side of the world. The transcontinental railroad across the USA, the gold-rushes in California and Australia, the "Underground" railroad system in London, all of these works required explosives. However, there were only two main explosives in the mid 19th century which were unstable and hard to control. The black powder and Nitroglycerine.

In 1860, the Swedish industrialist, engineer, and inventor, Alfred Nobel started his invention of dynamite. Nobel understood that Nitroglycerin is powerful but in its natural liquid state, it is very volatile. Nobel started his research on Nitroglycerin and discovered that by mixing nitroglycerine and silica, it turns into a malleable paste which he called it "dynamite" later on. In 1866, he first invented the dynamite successfully.

Dynamite became very popular because construction workers and engineers then had a powerful and safe explosive. Without the dynamite, the industrial revolution might still be successful but would for sure had much more injuries and probably would take a longer time.

As we all know, dynamite was not always confined to industrial purposes only. It was also used for murder and assassination plots. What a shame when you have the right product on the wrong person's hand. Because of publicity like that, Nobel decided to create the famous Nobel prizes that now bear his name.

炸藥

炸藥來自希臘字「DYNAMIS」，意思是「力量」。

　　第 18 和 19 世紀被稱為西方社會工業革命的景氣年。橫跨美國橫貫大陸的鐵路正在修建，在澳洲及加州的淘金熱，及在倫敦的「Underground」鐵路系統，正在興建。所有這些工程都需要爆炸物。然而在 19 世紀中期只有兩種不穩定且難以控制的主要爆炸物：黑火藥和硝化甘油。1860 年，瑞典實業家、工程師和發明家，諾貝爾開始了他的炸藥發明。諾貝爾了解，硝酸甘油是強大的，但在它的自然液體狀態是非常不穩定的。諾貝爾開始了他對硝酸甘油的研究。他發現通過混合硝酸甘油和二氧化矽，會變化為一個黏土的狀態，他將之命名為

「炸藥」。1866 年他第一次成功地發明了炸藥。

炸藥變得非常流行。因為建築工人和工程師可以有一個強大且安全的爆發物。沒有炸藥，工業革命依然可能成功，但將肯定有更多的傷患，也可能需要較長的時間。

大家都知道，炸藥並不只用於工業用途。它也被用於謀殺和暗殺。當正確的東西落在錯誤的人手裡，這是令人惋惜的。由於這樣的負面宣傳，諾貝爾決定創建著名的諾貝爾獎，並以他為名。

必考字彙表

字彙	詞形	中譯	反義詞	中譯
Dynamite	*n.*	炸藥		
Boom	*n.*	暴漲 激增	Decline	降低
Revolution	*n.*	革命	Stagnation	停滯
Transcontinental	*adj.*	橫貫大陸的		
System	*n.*	系統	Fraction	片段
Explosive	*adj.*	爆炸性的	Stable	安定的
Unstable	*adj.*	不安定的	Calm	安定的
Nitroglycerine	*n.*	硝化甘油		
Industrialist	*n.*	工業家		
Volatile	*adj.*	易揮發的	Placid	平穩的
Silica	*n.*	二氧化矽		
Malleable	*adj.*	具延展性的	Rigid	堅硬的
Paste	*n.*	糊狀物		

Construction	*n.*	建設	Destruction	消滅
Murder	*n.*	謀殺		
Assassination	*n.*	暗殺		
Shame	*adj.*	可恥的	Honorable	光榮的

Alfred Nobel MP3 40

Alfred Nobel was the fourth son of Immanuel Nobel and Carolina Andriette Nobel. His father, Immanuel Nobel was an inventor as well; therefore, while growing up, Alfred Nobel was given a lot of freedom to do experiments and eventually became an inventor himself.

Nobel was born in Stockholm, Sweden on October 21st, 1833. His family moved to St. Petersburg in Russia in 1842. Nobel was sent to private tutoring, and he excelled in his studies, particularly in chemistry and languages. He achieved fluency in English, French, German and Russian. Thru out his life, Nobel only went to school for 18 months.

In 1860, Nobel started his invention of dynamite, and it was 1866 when he first invented the dynamite successfully. Nobel never let himself take any rests. He founded Nitroglycerin AB in Stockholm, Sweden in 1864. A year later, he built the Alfred Nobel & Co. Factory in Hamburg,

01
Part
飲食民生

02
Part
歷史懷舊

03
Part
現代實用科技

04
Part
資訊知識

Germany. In 1866, he established the United States Blasting Oil Company in the U.S. And 4 years later, he established the Société général pour la fabrication de la dynamite in Paris, France.

Nobel was proud to say he is a world citizen. He passed away in 1896. A year before that, he started the Nobel prize which is awarded yearly to people whose work helps humanity. When he died, Alfred Nobel left behind a nine-million-dollar endowment fund.

阿爾弗雷德・諾貝爾

阿爾弗雷德・諾貝爾是伊曼紐爾 諾貝爾和卡羅來納 安德烈特 諾貝爾的第四個兒子。他的父親，伊曼紐爾 諾貝爾是一位發明家；因此，在成長過程中，諾貝爾被賦予了很多自由做實驗，並最終成為一個發明家。

諾貝爾於 1833 年 10 月 21 日出生在瑞典斯德哥爾摩。在 1842 年時，他舉家遷往俄羅斯聖彼得堡。諾貝爾被送往私塾，他擅長於學習，特別是在化學和語言。他能精通英語，法語，德語和俄語。終其一生，諾貝爾只去了學校 18 個月。

1860 年，諾貝爾開始了炸藥的發明。1866 年，他第一次成功地發明了炸藥。諾貝爾從來沒有讓自己休息。他於 1864 年在瑞典斯德哥爾

摩創立硝酸甘油 **AB** 公司。一年後，他在德國漢堡建立了阿爾弗雷德・諾貝爾公司的工廠。**1866** 年，他在美國成立了美國爆破石油公司。**4** 年後，他又在法國巴黎成立了炸藥實驗室。

諾貝爾自豪地説，他是一個世界公民。他在 **1896** 年過世。在他過世前，他成立諾貝爾獎以鼓勵對人類有幫助的人們 。當他過世時，諾貝爾留下了九百萬美元的捐贈基金。

字彙

字彙	詞形	中譯	反義詞	中譯
Freedom	*n.*	自由	Restriction	限制
Experiment	*n.*	實驗		
Tutoring	*v.*	私淑學習		
Excel	*v.*	勝過他人	Fall behind	落後
Particularly	*adv.*	特別	Usually	一般地
Achieve	*v.*	完成	Fail	失敗
Fluency	*n.*	流利	Hesitancy	躊躇
Establish	*v.*	創立	Close down	倒閉
Blast	*n.*	爆破	Construct	建設
Fabrication	*n.*	製造	Destruction	破壞
Prize	*n.*	獎		
Humanity	*n.*	人道	Cruelty	殘酷
Endowment	*n.*	捐贈的基金		

01
Part
飲食民生

02
Part
歷史懷舊

03
Part
現代實用科技

04
Part
資訊知識

20-2 試題演練

牛刀小試

1. The French _____ changed France from a monarchy to a republic.

   A. Evaluation   B. Revolution

   C. Destination   D. Recreation

2. The freeway is shut down due to a development of an _____ device.

   A. boom   B. explore

   C. bomb   D. explosive

3. Food and fuel prices are very _____ in a war situation.

   A. expensive   B. volatile

   C. stable   D. low

4. Lead was being used widely in construction during the 90s because it is _____ metal and cheap.

   A. stiff   B. hard

   C. liquid   D. malleable

5. It is a _____ to have racial discrimination.

    A. shame   B. honor

    C. idea   D. thought

6. The German team had _____ themselves and won the world champion last year.

    A. become   B. pursued

    C. excelled   D. over

7. Not many people apply for the job because one of the requirements of the job is _____ in English and Korean.

    A. fluent   B. frequent

    C. fluency   D. frequency

8. In order for his daughter to enter the school, he made an _____ of 50,000 dollars to the library.

    A. donate   B. purchase

    C. donation   D. endowment

01
Part
飲食民生

02
Part
歷史懷舊

03
Part
現代實用科技

04
Part
資訊知識

1. **(B)** 由於句意是在形容法國大革命，因此解答應為 revolution A 選項 evaluation 評估，C 選項 destination 目的地，D 選項 recreation 娛樂均不符合句意。

2. **(D)** 空格應填寫形容 device 的形容詞，因此可以簡單選出 explosive 為解答 A 選項 boom 繁榮，B 選項 explore 探索，C 選項 bomb 炸彈均不符合。

3. **(B)** 在戰爭時，物價及油價都是「易變的」，所以解答為 volatile。

4. **(D)** 此空格應選擇形容可塑性金屬的形容詞，因此 malleable 是正確答案。表示鉛於 90 年代廣泛地用於建築物上，因為其是可塑性高的金屬且便宜 A 選項 stiff 僵硬的，B 選項 hard 硬的，C 選項 liquid 液態的均不符合。

5. **(A)** 由 Discrimination 這個字可以清楚的理解答案應為 shame。

6. **(C)** 由句意可以理解應填寫含有「超越「含義的字詞，因此解答為 excelled 表示德國隊已自我超越且於去年贏得世界盃，A 選項 become，B 選項 pursued，D 選項 over 均不符合文意。

7. (C) 空格需填入名詞，故刪去 a 和 b，且由句意可以理解只有
fluency 符合答案需求，表示很少人申請這個工作因為這個職
缺的需求是流暢的英文和韓文。

8. (D) 空格需填入名詞，所以 a 和 b 可以先刪除。而由句意可以理
解 endowment 是正確解答。Endowment 有才能、天賦的
意思，也有贈與…財產等給人的意思。此處為他為了讓他女兒
進此學校就讀，贈與五萬元給圖書館。

01
Part
飲食民生

02
Part
歷史懷舊

03
Part
現代實用科技

04
Part
資訊知識

Unit 21 21-1
Plastic
塑膠
by *Leo Baekeland*

 **Plastic** MP3 41

Although different types of pollutions caused by plastic have been public issues for years, it seems hard to get rid of plastic for its relatively low production cost, versatility and imperviousness to water. From grocery bags to toys to even clothes, plastics are used in an enormous and expanding range of products. It is also being widely used in the medical field and construction field.

The very first plastic material was discovered by Charles Goodyear's during the discovery of vulcanization to thermoset materials derived from natural rubber in the 1800s. After that, many scientists contributed to the discovery of different types of plastics. It was not until 1907, a scientist Leo Baekeland invented "Bakelite" which was the first fully synthetic plastic. He also was the person who coined the term "Plastics." The rapid growth in chemical technology led to the invention of many new forms of plastics, such as Polystyrene, Polyvinyl chloride, and polyethylene

Many traditional materials, such as wood, stone, leather,

ceramic that we normally used in the past were replaced by plastics.

What is plastics exactly? The majority of the polymers are based on chains of carbon atoms alone with oxygen, sulfur, or nitrogen. Most plastics contain other organic or inorganic compounds blended in. The amount of additives ranges from zero percentage to more than 50% for certain electronic applications.

The invention of plastic was a great success but also brought us a serious environmental concerns regarding its slow decomposition rate after being discarded. One way to help with the environment is to practice recycling or use other environmental friendly materials instead. Another approach is to speed up the development of biodegradable plastic.

01
Part
飲食民生

02
Part
歷史懷舊

03
Part
現代實用科技

04
Part
資訊知識

塑膠

　　雖然因為塑膠所造成的各種污染已是多年來的公共問題，但由於生產成本相對低廉，具通用性及抗滲水性，因此我們似乎無法擺脫這種材料。從食品塑膠袋到玩具，甚至服裝，塑膠產品的範圍不斷擴大。它也被廣泛應用於醫療領域和建築領域。

史上第一個塑膠材料是在 1800 年代由查爾斯・固特異在天然橡膠的熱固性材料中發現的硫化物。

　　在此之後，許多科學家促成了不同類型塑膠的發現。直到 1907 年，科學家利奧・貝克蘭發明了酚醛塑料，這是第一個完全合成的塑膠。他也是命名「塑膠」的人。化學技術的極速成長導致許多形式的塑膠發明，例如聚苯乙烯、聚氯乙烯和聚乙烯。

　　塑膠到底是什麼？大多數聚合物都基於碳原子和氧，硫，或氮的鏈。大多數塑膠混有其他有機或無機化合物。在一些電子應用上，添加劑的量從零至 50％以上。

　　塑膠的發明獲得了巨大的成功，但也給我們帶來了關於其被丟棄後緩慢分解所造成嚴重的環境問題。練習回收或改用其他對環境友好的材料是幫助環境的一種方法。另一種方法是，加快生物分解性塑料的開發。

必考字彙表

字彙	詞形	中譯	反義詞	中譯
Versatility	*n.*	多用途	Limited	有限的
Imperviousness	*n.*	透不過	Responsiveness	易起反應的
Construction	*n.*	建造	Destruction	破壞
Vulcanization	*n.*	橡膠的硫化		
Thermoset	*n.*	熱固性		
Derive	*v.*	衍生出	Forfeit	喪失

Contribute	*v.*	貢獻	Counteract	妨礙
Synthetic	*adj.*	假想的	Genuine	真的
Majority	*n.*	多數	Minority	少數
Polymer	*n.*	聚合物		
Carbon	*n.*	碳		
Organic	*adj.*	有機的	Inorganic	非有機的
Additive	*adj.*	附加的		
Environmental	*adj.*	環境的		
Decomposition	*n.*	分解	Unification	聯合
Biodegradable	*adj.*	可生物分解的		

01 Part 飲食民生

02 Part 歷史懷舊

03 Part 現代實用科技

04 Part 資訊知識

Leo Baekeland MP3 42

The father of the Plastics Industry, Leo Baekeland, was born in Belgium on November 14th, 1863. He was best known for his invention of Bakelite which is an inexpensive, nonflammable and versatile plastic. Because of his invention, the plastic industry started to bloom and became a popular material in many different industries.

Baekeland acquired a PhD. in chemistry in the University of Ghent and became an associate professor there. He and his wife traveled to New York in 1889 and got a job offer by Richard Anthony who owned a photographic company. Baekeland worked there for 2 years and formed his own business as a consultant. This job didn't last long though. He eventually went back to his old interest of producing a photographic paper that would allow enlargements to be printed by artificial lights. After 2 years of efforts, he invented the first commercial photographic paper "Velox".

After inventing Velox, Baekeland set another goal to develop something that would bring him fortune the quickest way possible. Baekeland began to investigate the reactions of phenol and formaldehyde. As always, Baekeland approached the field systematically. He carefully controlled all his work and examed the effects of temperature, pressure and all possible factors. In 1907, he proudly made his dream plastic-Bakelite. Later, he received many awards and medals, and passed away in 1944.

利奧・貝克蘭

塑膠工業之父，利奧・貝克蘭，於 1863 年 11 月 14 日出生於比利時。他最為人知的是酚醛塑的發明，這是一種廉價，不可燃和通用的塑膠。由於他的發明，塑料行業開始盛行，在許多不同的行業成為一個受歡迎的材料。

貝克蘭在根特大學攻讀化學並取得化學博士學位，並成為該校特約化學副教授。他和他的妻子在 1889 年前往了紐約，並在理查德・安東尼所擁有的攝影公司裡得到一個工作機會。貝克蘭在那裡工作了 2 年後，組織了自己的顧問公司。但這項工作並沒有持續多久，他最終又回到他舊有的興趣，允許放大到人工燈光打印的相紙開發。經過 2 年的努力，他發明了第一個商業相紙「Velox」。

發明 Velox 後，貝克蘭訂了另外一個目標，這個目標是要是發明出可以以最快的速度賺取更多的錢的東西。貝克蘭開始調查苯酚和甲醛的反應。與往常一樣，貝克蘭有系統地小心控管溫度，壓力和所有可能的因素，並測試各種反應。 1907 年，他自豪地做了他的夢想塑膠 - 酚醛塑。之後，他獲得了許多獎章和榮譽並於 1944 年離開人世。

字彙

字彙	詞形	中譯	反義詞	中譯
Nonflammable	*adj.*	不易燃的	Inflammable	可燃的
Versatile	*adj.*	多功能的	Inept	無能的
Acquire	*v.*	取得	Disperse	消失
Associate	*n.*	合夥人	Foe	敵人
Photographic	*adj.*	攝影的		
Enlargement	*n.*	擴大	Compression	壓縮
Artificial	*adj.*	人造的	Natural	自然的
Investigate	*v.*	調查	Overlook	漏看
Phenol	*n.*	酚		
Formaldehyde	*n.*	甲醛		
Approach	*v.*	接近	Retreat	撤退
Systematically	*adv.*	有系統地	Haphazardly	偶然地

01
Part
飲食民生

02
Part
歷史懷舊

03
Part
現代實用科技

04
Part
資訊知識

21-2 試題演練

牛刀小試

1. The tourist industry is growing rapidly, creating a _____ boom for hotels.

   A. construction   B. concrete
   C. purchasing   D. destruction

2. As famous as he is, he _____ a lot of time and money to helping homeless people.

   A. donation   B. contribution
   C. donator   D. contributes

3. The _____ of songs sung by the Beatles were composed by John Lennon.

   A. most   B. popular
   C. majority   D. top

4. This planet could be on the brink of an _____ disaster if we don't stop the pollution.

   A. seriously   B. earth
   C. globe   D. environmental

5. Clothes should not be made of _____ material.

   A. unflammable   B. firable

   C. inflammable   D. flame

6. The government just passed the plan to _____ the exhibition hall.

   A. enlargement   B. increase

   C. recreation   D. enlarge

7. Several medical reports have shown that gums with ____ sweeteners cause cancer.

   A. natural   B. artificial

   C. naturally   D. artificially

8. Most companies don't like the government _____ to go thru the financial records because they might raise many questions.

   A. checkers   B. investigators

   C. officers   D. investigation

01
Part
飲食民生

02
Part
歷史懷舊

03
Part
現代實用科技

04
Part
資訊知識

 題目解析

1. (A) Boom 前面應加名詞。而前句的 growing rapidly 說明了建設的需要，因此答案為 construction。表示觀光業的快速發展創造了旅館的建築榮景，B 選項 concrete，C 選項 purchasing，D 選項 destruction 均不符合文意。

2. (D) 空格應加入動詞，因此 contributes 為正確答案 A 選項 donation，B 選項 contribution C 選項 donator 均不符合。

3. (C) 空格應填入名詞，因此解答為 majority。指大多數 the Beatles 所唱的歌曲是由 John Lennon 作曲的。

4. (D) 空格應填入形容 disaster 的形容詞，因此 environmental 為適當的答案 A 選項 seriously，B 選項 earth，C 選項 globe 均不符合。

5. (C) Firable 不存在，因此可先刪除 b。而空白處應填入「可燃的」形容詞，因此 inflammable 為正確答案。表示衣物不該是由易燃材質製成的。

6. (D) to 之後應加動詞，a 和 c 分別為 ment 和 tion 結尾，因此可先刪除 a 和 c。又由句意可選出 enlarge 為正確答案。

7. (B) 空格應填入形容詞而 C 選項 naturally 天然地和 D 選項 artifically 人工地均為副詞故不符合，句尾又提及 _____ 會造成癌症，因此解答為 artificial。

8. (B) 由句意可以得知空白處應填入一個職位，investigators 為最適當的選項 A 選項 checkers，C 選項 officers，D 選項 investigation 均不符合。

01 Part 飲食民生

02 Part 歷史懷舊

03 Part 現代實用科技

04 Part 資訊知識

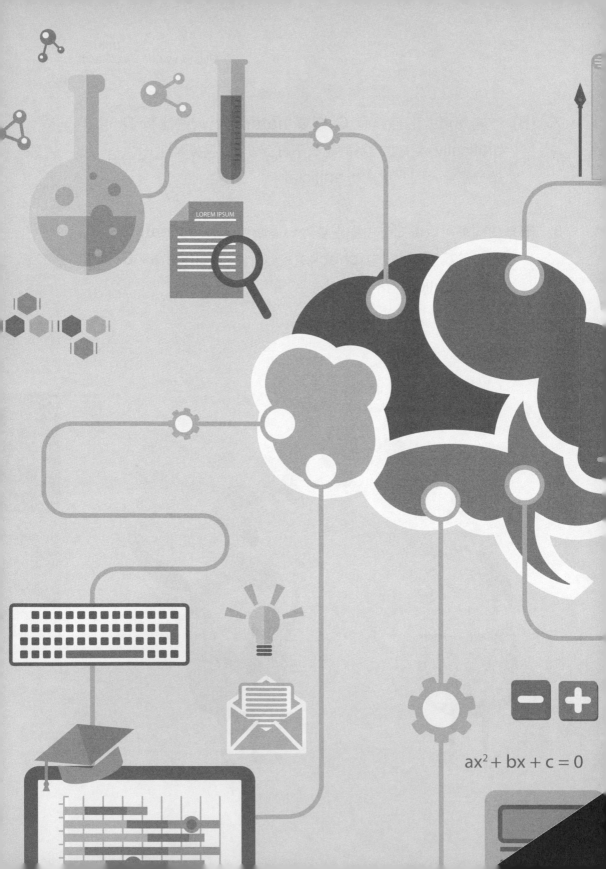

Part 4
資訊知識

Unit 22 22-1
Barcode
條碼
by *Bernard Silver and Norman Joseph Woodland*

Barcode MP3 43

Infinity amount of information is being stored by these lines or dots. They limited human errors and fastened the transit of information. But when we are doing the easy scanning, have we even considered this-What exactly is a barcode? How does it work?

A barcode is an optical machine-readable representation of data relating to the object to which it is attached. We see it on almost all products. Originally, barcodes systematically represented data by varying the widths and spacing of parallel lines. Now we even have the two dimensional barcodes that evolved into rectangles, dots, hexagons and other patterns.

Also nowadays, we no longer require special optical scanners to read the barcodes. They can be read by smartphones as well.

The idea of the creation came from a graduate student named Bernard Silver at Drexel Institute of Technology in

Philadelphia, Pennsylvania in 1948. He overheard the request from the president of the local food chain. He immediately saw the demand for the system and then stated the development with his friend Norman Joseph Woodland who also went to Drexel. Woodland later of left Drexel and kept his research in Florida. He got the inspiration from Morse code first and then he adapted technology from optical soundtracks in movies in order to read them. The patent for Barcode was filed as "Classifying Apparatus and Method" on October 20th, 1949 by the both of them. Later on, IBM offered to buy the patent but the offer was too low. Philco later on purchased the patent in 1962 with 15,000 dollars and then sold it to RCA sometime later.

條碼

　　無限量的信息被存儲在這些線或點裡。他們將人為錯誤減到最低並加快了訊息的傳訊。但是，當我們在做這簡單的掃描時，我們是否有想過 - 到底什麼是條碼？它是如何作業的？

　　條碼是一個光學儀器可讀取有關連結對象的數據。我們幾乎可以在所有產品上看到它。最初是通過改變寬度和平行線間距的條碼系統來表示數據。現在，我們甚至有利用矩形、點、六邊形等所演變出的二維條碼。而且現在，我們不再需要特殊的光學掃描儀讀取條碼。它們可以通過智能電話被讀取。

這個創作的想法來自一個在賓州費城的 Drexel 技術學院就讀的研究生-伯納德‧史維。他當時無意間聽到當地的連鎖食品店老闆的要求。他立即看到了這個系統的需求，於是他找了也在 Drexel 就讀的朋友-諾曼‧伍德蘭一起開發這個系統。後來伍德蘭離開了 Drexel，到了佛羅里達繼續他的開發。他從摩斯密碼得到靈感，爾後再改編電影配樂的技術以便讀取它們。條碼的專利在 1949 年 10 月 20 日被以「分級裝置和方法」的方式由兩位共同提出。後來 IBM 提出購買該專利的要求，但報價太低。Philco 在 1962 年以 15,000 美元買下專利，並爾後將其賣給了 RCA。

必考字彙表

字彙	詞性	中譯	反義詞	中譯
Infinity	*n.*	無限	Limitation	限制
Transit	*v.*	傳送	Stagnation	停滯
Consider	*v.*	考慮	Disregard	忽視
Optical	*adj.*	光學的		
Representation	*n.*	代表		
Object	*n.*	物體		
Systematically	*adv.*	有系統地	Haphazardly	隨意的
Parallel	*adj.*	平行的	Vertical	垂直的
Dimensional	*adj.*	次元的		
Evolve	*v.*	發展	Diminish	削弱
Rectangle	*n.*	矩形		
Hexagon	*n.*	六角形		
Overhear	*v.*	無意間聽到		

Inspiration	*n.*	靈感		
Adapt	*v.*	使適應	Disarrange	使混亂
Classify	*v.*	分類	Combine	合併
Apparatus	*n.*	設備		

Bernard Silver & Norman Joseph Woodland

Two students from Drexel Institute of Technology, Bernard Silver and Norman Joseph Woodland jointly developed the barcode technology.

Silver overheard the system request from an owner of a local chain store and started his barcode development with Norman Joseph Woodland. He later on served as a physics instructor at Drexel. Unfortunately, Silver passed away on August 28th, 1963 due to leukemia. He was only 38.

Before studying in Mechanical Engineering at Drexel Institute of Technology, Woodland did military service in World War II as a technical assistant in Tennessee. After having earned his Bachelor degree from Drexel, he also worked as a lecturer in mechanical engineer in the same school.

Silver and Woodland started the barcode development

in 1948. Woodland then quit his teaching job and moved to Florida to concentrate on his research on the system. The two of them applied for a patent on October 20, 1949 and received U.S patent 2 years later. The pattern covered both linear and circular bulls eye printing designs. In 2011 Silver, alongside Woodland, was inducted into the National Inventors Hall of Fame. A year later, Woodland passed away from the effects of Alzheimer's disease.

伯納德・史維與諾曼・喬瑟夫・伍德蘭

兩名 Drexel 的研究生，伯納德・史維－出生於 1924 年 9 月 21 日和諾曼・喬瑟夫・伍德蘭－出生於 1921 年 9 月 6 日，聯合開發了條碼技術。

當時，他從當地連鎖店的老闆聽到了系統的要求，於是與諾曼・伍德蘭開始了條碼的發展。他後來在 Drexel 擔任物理教師。不幸的是，史維在 1963 年 8 月 28 日因白血病過世。當時他只有 38 歲。

在 Drexel 就讀機械工程系前，伍德蘭在二次世界大戰中服役，在美國田納西州擔任一個技術助理。獲得了他的學士學位後，他還在 Drexel 擔任機械工程師及講師。

史維和伍德蘭在 1948 年時開始了條碼的研究，伍德蘭並在 1948 年時辭掉教師工作，搬到佛羅里達州以專注於他的系統研究。他們倆在

1949 年 10 月 20 日申請了專利，並在兩年後獲得了美國專利。該專利涵蓋了直線和圓靶心的印刷設計。2011 年史維與伍德蘭被列入美國國家發明家名人堂。一年後，伍德蘭因阿茲海默症而過世。

字彙

字彙	詞形	中譯	反義詞	中譯
Institute	*n.*	學會		
Joint	*adj.*	聯合的	Individual	獨立的
Serve	*v.*	服役	Refrain	戒除
Physics	*n.*	物理學		
Leukemia	*n.*	白血病		
Mechanical	*adj.*	機械的	Manual	手動的
Military	*adj.*	軍事的	Civilian	平民百姓
Lecturer	*n.*	講師	Student	學生
Concentrate	*v.*	集中	Disperse	疏散
Linear	*adj.*	直線的		
Circular	*adj.*	環狀的		
Bulls eye	*n.*	靶心		
Alongside	*adv.*	並排地	Away	遠離
Induct	*v.*	引進	Reject	抵制
Alzheimer	*n.*	阿茲海默症		

01
Part
飲食民生

02
Part
歷史懷舊

03
Part
現代實用科技

04
Part
資訊知識

22-2 試題演練

牛刀小試

1. She requires all her teachers to have _____ patience with the children in the kindergarten.

   A. limited   B. infinity
   C. big   D. minimum

2. In _____ of others please do not put your feet on the chairs in front of you.

   A. considering   B. consider
   C. considered   D. consideration

3. The sociological theory states that human beings are ___ taught how to behave, feel, and think.

   A. automatically   B. systematically
   C. instantly   D. self learned

4. The three _____ function should be the standard for the next generation cell phones.

   A. degree   B. dimensional
   C. depth   D. angles

5. Anthony Robbins once said that you must have either _____ or desperation in life.

   A. creation   B. imagination
   C. inspiration   D. transportation

6. The data is _____, and can only be seen with authorization.

   A. locked   B. separated
   C. excluded   D. classified

7. Husband and wife normally have a _____ bank account that they can both deposit their paychecks into.

   A. double   B. join
   C. duplicate   D. joint

8. The Earth's orbit around the sun is not perfectly _____. It is slightly oval-shaped.

   A. circle   B. round
   C. ball shaped D. circular

1. **(B)** 由句意可推測應填入「極大的」一詞，因此 infinity 最為恰當。

2. **(D)** In _____ of 中空格處需填入名詞，因此解答為 consideration，A 選項 considering 為動名詞或現在分詞，B 選項 consider 為動詞，C 選項為動詞或過去分詞均不符合。

3. **(B)** 此處需填副詞，並由句意可推測 systematically 最為恰當，A 選項 automatically 自動地，C 選項 instantly 立即地，D 選項 self learned 均不符合，表示社會學理論聲稱人類受系統式地教育著如何表現、感覺和思考。

4. **(B)** 此處需填入形容詞，且只有 b 選項為形容詞，故由句意可推測 dimensional 為正確答案，表示Anthony Robbins曾說過生命中你必須有靈感或絕望。

5. **(C)** 四個選項均為名詞但由句意可簡單地挑選出 inspiration 為正確答案。

6. **(D)** 句尾的 can only be seen with authorization 說明了這個文件的隱密性，因此答案為 classified，表示資料是列入機密文件的，此為 classified 較特別的用法。

7. (D).此處需填入形容詞，b 和 c 為動詞故可以刪去，並由句意可推測 joint 最為恰當。表示丈夫跟妻子通常有共同的銀行帳戶，所以他們都能夠將款項存入。

8. (D) 依句構，句子中有主詞和主要動詞其後加 not 和副詞 perfectly 其後只能加形容詞，且當形容軌跡時，英語慣用 circular，因此為正確答案。

Unit 23　23-1
Google
谷歌

by *Larry Page and Sergey Brin*

Google　MP3 45

If you ever watched the movie "The Internship", you would be envied yet threatened by the people working for Google. A facility that gathered the most intelligent people from all fields around the world, Google gives its employees the best benefits, yet the most innovative and challenging jobs. People might ask, what does Google do? What is Google?

Google Inc. is an American multinational technology company. Google is not so much a company that invented one product as a company that invents anything relating to Internet. Starting from Google's core search engine, it also offers email service-Gmail, a cloud storage service- Google drive, Web browser-Google Chrome, to an even innovative hardware like Google glasses. The Google self-driving car is also being invented for years, and they plan to release it to the market in year 2020.

Google was founded as a private company in 1998 by Larry Page and Sergey Brin while they were Ph.D. students

01
Part
飲食民生

02
Part
歷史懷舊

03
Part
現代實用科技

04
Part
資訊知識

at Stanford University. An initial public offering followed on August 19, 2004. The company mission was to organize the world's information and made it universally accessible and useful. No doubt, they accomplished their mission and went much further. From the data in 2009, it processes over one billion search requests and about 24 petabytes of user-generated data each day as of 2009. Google.com should have been the most visited website in the world for years.

The headquarters of Google is located in Mountain View, California. They named it Googleplex. They moved into the facility the same year when the company went IPO in 2004. The company offered 19,605,052 shares at a price of $85 per share. By January 2014, its market capitalization had grown to $397 billion.

谷歌

如果你看過電影「實習大叔」，你必然既羨慕又感覺被為谷歌工作的人所威脅。該公司集合了世界各個領域的頂尖聰明人，谷歌給員工最好的福利，也是最具創新性和挑戰性的工作。人們可能會問，谷歌是做什麼的？什麼是谷歌？

谷歌是美國的跨國科技公司。與其說谷歌發明了一種產品，還不如說是谷歌發明所有涉及到互聯網的產品。從谷歌的核心搜索引擎開始，它也提供電子郵件服務 – Gmail、雲存儲服務 – Google Drive、網絡瀏覽器- Google Chrome，甚至創新的硬件，如谷歌眼鏡。谷歌自動駕駛汽車也被開發多年，他們計劃在 2020 年發布到市場。

　　谷歌是於 1998 年由拉里・佩奇和謝爾蓋・布林在史丹佛大學攻讀他們博士學位時所創立的私人公司。隨後於 2004 年 8 月 19 日首次上市。該公司的使命是整合全球信息，使人人皆可使用並從中受益。毫無疑問，他們完成了他們的使命，且更進一步。根據 2009 年的數據，它的搜索器處理超過十億個搜索請求，用戶每天約 24 PB 的量。Google.com 多年來應該都是世界上訪問量最大的網站。

　　谷歌的總部設在加州山景城。他們把它命名為 Googleplex。他們在 2004 年搬進了這棟建築，同時並首次公開發行。該公司以 85 美元美股的金額提供了 19605052 股。到 2014 年 1 月，其市值已增長到 3970 億美元。

必考字彙表

字彙	詞形	中譯	反義詞	中譯
Internship	*n.*	實習		
Envy	*v.*	嫉妒	Goodwill	友好
Threaten	*v.*	威脅	Reassure	使放心
Benefit	*n.*	津貼	Detriment	損傷
Challenging	*adj.*	挑戰性的	Easy	簡單的
Multinational	*adj.*	跨國的	National	國家的

Core	*n.*	核心	Exterior	外部的
Cloud	*n.*	雲端		
Browser	*n.*	瀏覽器		
Hardware	*n.*	硬體	Software	軟體
Initial	*adj.*	起初的	Final	最終的
Universally	*adv.*	通用地	Locally	局部地
Accomplish	*v.*	完成	Begin	開始
Process	*n.*	程序		
Capitalization	*n.*	資本額		

Larry Page and Sergey Brin

MP3 46

Larry Page:

Being a child of two computer experts, Larry Page was born in an environment that led him to who he is today. Born in 1973, Page grew up in a standard home that was filled with computers and technical and science magazines in Michigan. He first played with a computer at the age of six and immediately got attracted to it. He was the first kid who utilized a word processor to do his homework. He was also encouraged by his family to take things apart to see how they work. Maybe that's why he got interested in inventing things.

Page earned his Bachelor degree in engineering from the University of Michigan and concentrated on computer engineering at Stanford University where he met his partner Sergey Brin.

Sergey Brin:

A Russian-born American, Sergey Brin immigrated to the United States with his family from the Soviet Union at the age of 6. His father wanted to give Brin an environment where it allowed Brin to get good education and able to proceed his dream. Brin followed his father's and grandfather's footsteps by studying mathematics and computer science. He earned his bachelor's degree at the University of Maryland.

He then moved to Stanford University to acquire a PhD in computer science.

The birth of Google:

Page and Brin met at an orientation for new students at Stanford. They became close friends after having a disagreement on most subjects. The two of them authored a paper titled "The Anatomy of a Large-Scale Hypertextual Web Search Engine" together.

They created a search engine that listed results according to the popularity of the pages. It was the basic form of Google Search. They came up with the name "Google" from the mathematical term "googol". It reflects their mission to organize the humongous amount information on the internet. The program became popular so both of them suspended their PhD studies. Just like HP and Apple, the company started from a garage.

 ## 拉里・佩奇與謝爾蓋・布林

拉里・佩奇：

父母皆為電腦專家，拉里・佩奇出生的環境造就了他。出生於 1973 年，佩琪在密西根一個充滿電腦和技術及科學雜誌的標準家庭中長大。在他六歲的時候，他開始玩他的第一台電腦，並立即被吸引。他是在他上的小學裡第一個利用文字處理器做功課的小孩。他的家人也鼓勵他拆解東西來看看是如何運作的。也許這就是為什麼他對發明創造有興趣。

佩琪從密歇根大學得到了他的工程學位。之後，他便在史丹佛大學專心於他的資訊工程學位。在那裡他遇到了他的搭檔謝爾蓋・布林。

謝爾蓋・布林：

俄國出生的美國人，謝爾蓋‧布林在六歲時與他的家人一起由蘇聯移民到美國。他的父親想給布林一個良好的教育環境，能夠繼續他的夢想的環境。布林跟隨父親和祖父的腳步學習數學和資訊工程。他在馬里蘭大學獲得了學士學位。

爾後，他到史丹佛大學研讀資訊工程博士學位。

谷歌的誕生：

佩奇和布林在史丹佛大學的一個新生訓練上認識。他們在不同意對方大部分的意見後不久，變成親密的朋友。他們倆一同撰寫題為「大規模網絡搜索引擎剖析」的論文。

他們當時創立了一個根據網頁的普及率來列出結果的搜索引擎。這是谷歌搜索的基本形式。他們以數學術語「天文數字」這個詞想出「谷歌」這個名字。這反映了他們的使命，即是組織規劃在互聯網上堆積如山量的訊息。由於這個程式很受歡迎，因此他們都暫停了攻讀博士學位。就像惠普與蘋果電腦，該公司是從一個車庫開始的。

必考字彙表

字彙	詞形	中譯	反義詞	中譯
Expert	n.	專家	Amateur	業餘者
Technical	adj.	技術性的	General	一般的
Assignment	n.	功課		

Encourage	*v.*	鼓勵	Discourage	使沮喪
Concentrate	*v.*	全神貫注		
Proceed	*v.*	繼續進行	Recede	後退
Footstep	*n.*	腳步		
Mathematics	*n.*	數學		
Orientation	*n.*	新生訓練		
Disagreement	*n.*	意見不合	Agreement	同意
Author	*v.*	編寫		
Popularity	*n.*	大眾化		
Googol	*n.*	天文數字	One	一
Humongous	*adj.*	巨大無比的	Tiny	極小的

23-2 試題演練

牛刀小試

1. In the United States, it is very important for students to enter an _____ program after college. It helps finding a good job in the future.

   A. graduate   B. internship
   C. internet   D. computer

2. The kidnapper _____ to kill the boy if his demands were not met.

   A. considered   B. thought
   C. threatened   D. committed

3. It is his dream to work in a _____ company which allows him to use his bilingual ability.

   A. national   B. internationally
   C. multinational   D. multibillion

4. No matter what you do, you should work hard in order to _____ your goal.

    A. accommodate   B. achieved

    C. end   D. accomplish

5. Due to _____ issues, the flight will be delayed.

    A. technician   B. technically

    C. technical   D. technicality

6. She is grateful that she was _____ by her parents to learn piano at the age of three.

    A. forced   B. interesting

    C. encouraged   D. bored

7. During _____ week, the new students will be introduced to all the facilities available to them during their studies here.

    A. training   B. orientation

    C. operational   D. introduce

8. Recently _____ burgers are popular in Taiwan which created a lot of food waste.

    A. tasty   B. gourmet

    C. one dollar   D. humongous

 **題目解析**

1. **(B)** 在這個文句中,「實習」是最符合的選項,因此答案為 internship。其中 internship program 為常見用法。

2. **(C)** 主要子句中少了動詞,且由翻譯可得知 threatened 是最適合的選項。表示綁架者威脅要殺了男孩,如果沒達到他們的需求。

3. **(C)** 由文法來看,空格應填入形容詞,而句尾的 bilingual ability 說明了選項應為「跨國的」,因此 multinational 為正確選項。

4. **(D)** 空格應填入「達成目標」的原型動詞,因此 accomplish 為正確答案表示不論你做甚麼,你應該努力工作以達到你的目標。

5. **(C)** 空格應填入形容詞,因此 technical 為正確選項,表示由於技術性問題,班機將會延誤。

6. **(C)** 由句意判斷其為被動意思,且不該選 forced 因其為負面意思,與前面的 grateful 相牴觸,故由句意及字彙可以簡單選出 encouraged 為正確答案,表示她很感恩她在三歲時父母鼓勵她學習小提琴。

7. **(B)** 空格需填入「新生訓練」一詞,因此正確選項為 orientation。

8. (D) 字尾的 food waste 說明了空格應填入 humongous。
   Humongous 為正確選項。

01
Part
飲食民生

02
Part
歷史懷舊

03
Part
現代實用科技

04
Part
資訊知識

Unit 24 24-1
Facebook
臉書
by **Mark Zuckerberg**

MP3 47

Have you checked your Facebook? Are you friends with someone? These are some common questions that we ask one another everyday now. Some people are even addicted to Facebook so much that they could not stop checking it every 2 minutes. Hard to imagine that 10 years ago, this multi-billion business did not even exist.

Facebook was founded by Mark Zuckerberg and his roommates and friends at Harvard University in 2004. This social networking service was originally limited to Harvard students, and later on expanded to other colleges in the Boston area, the Ivy Leagues, and gradually most universities in Canada and the US. At that time, high school networks required an invitation to join. Facebook later expanded membership eligibility to employees of several companies, including Apple Inc. and Microsoft. It was not available to the public until September 26, 2006.

The popularity of Facebook started to generate in 2007. Most of the youngsters back then joined Facebook in 2007.

Late in 2007, Facebook had 100,000 business pages which allowed companies to attract potential customers and introduce themselves. The business potential for this social network just kept blooming, and on October 2008, Facebook set up its international headquarters in Dublin, Ireland.

Statistics from October 2011 showed that over 100 billion photos were shared on Facebook, and over 350 million users accessed Facebook through their mobile phones which is only about 33% of all Facebook traffic.

01
Part
飲食民生

02
Part
歷史懷舊

03
Part
現代實用科技

04
Part
資訊知識

臉書

你看了你的臉書了嗎？你跟這個人是朋友了嗎？這些都是一些我們現在在日常生活中會互相問的問題。有些人甚至非常沈迷於臉書，每 2 分鐘就要檢查一次。很難想像 10 年前，這個數十億的產業根本不存在。

臉書這個社交網路服務由馬克‧札克伯格和他的室友以及在哈佛大學的朋友在 2004 年時成立臉書這個社交網絡服務。最初僅限於哈佛學生使用，爾後擴大到波士頓地區的其他學校及常春藤聯盟。逐步的加入了大部分加拿大和美國的大學。當時，高中生是需要被邀請才能加入。臉書後來擴大會員資格給幾家大公司，包括蘋果公司和微軟公司的僱員。直到 2006 年 9 月 26 日才開放給社會大眾。

臉書於 2007 年開始普及。當時大部分的年輕人都是在 2007 年加入臉書。2007 年的下半年，臉書開始有企業專頁，使得企業可以介紹自己的企業並吸引潛在客戶。社會網絡的商業潛力不停地綻放。2008 年 10 月，臉書在愛爾蘭的都柏林設立了國際總部。

　　從 2011 年 10 月的統計顯示，超過一兆的照片在臉書上共享，而超過 350 萬的用戶利用手機查閱臉書，這大概只是 33%的臉書的總流量。

必考字彙表

字彙	詞性	中譯	反義詞	中譯
Common	adj.	常見的	Rare	不常見的
Addict	v.	上癮	Detract	使分心
Exist	v.	存在	Cease	停止
Social	adj.	社交的	Private	私人的
Networking	n.	建立關係網路		
Expand	v.	擴大	Contract	縮小
Gradually	adv.	逐步地	Rapidly	立即地
Popularity	n.	知名度	Infamy	惡名狼藉
Generate	v.	引起	Prevent	預防
Youngster	n.	年輕人	Elder	老年
Attract	v.	吸引	Disinterest	不關心
Bloom	v.	興盛	Wither	衰弱
Access	v.	進入	Egress	外出
Traffic	n.	交流量		

Mark Zuckerberg

MP3 48

Born in 1984, Mark Zuckerberg was born in White Plains, New York. Zuckerberg began using computers and writing software in middle school. His father taught him Atari BASIC Programming in the 1990s, and later hired software developer David Newman to tutor him privately. Zuckerberg took a graduate course in the subject at Mercy College near his home while still in high school. He enjoyed developing computer programs, especially communication tools and games.

When he studied classes Harvard, Zuckerberg had already achieved a "reputation as a programming prodigy", notes Vargas. In his sophomore year, he wrote a program he called CourseMatch, which allowed users to make class selection decisions based on the choices of other students and also to help them form study groups. A short time later, he created a different program he initially called Facemash that lets students select the best looking person from a choice.

On February 4, 2004, Zuckerberg launched "The facebook". Zuckerberg dropped out of Harvard in his sophomore year to complete his project. Once at college, Zuckerberg's Facebook started off as just a "Harvard thing" until Zuckerberg decided to spread it to other schools. After Zuckerberg moved to Palo Alto, California with Moskovitz and some friends, they leased a small house that served as an office. They got their first office in mid-2004. In 2007, at the age of 23, Zuckerberg became a billionaire as a result of Facebook's success. The number of Facebook users worldwide reached a total of one billion in 2012.

馬克・扎克伯格

1984 年，馬克・扎克伯格出生於紐約的懷特普萊恩斯。扎克伯格在中學時期就開始使用電腦和編寫的軟體。他的父親教他寫 90 年代的 Atari BASIC 編程，後來又聘請了軟體開發者大衛・紐曼私下指導他。扎克伯格在高中時便在他家附近的慈悲學院選修研究生的課程。他喜歡開發電腦軟體，特別是通訊工具和遊戲。

當他開始在哈佛就讀時，扎克伯格早已經取得了「程式撰寫神童」的美譽 Vargas 提到。在他大二那年，他寫了一個程式叫 CourseMatch，這個程式可以幫助學生選課，也幫助他們組成學習小組。不久之後，他創造了一個不同的程式，他最初取名為 Facemash 讓學生選擇最好看的人。

2004 年 2 月 4 日，扎克伯格推出了「The facebook」。扎克伯格在大二時從哈佛退學，以完成他的計劃。在大學裡時扎克伯格的臉書一開始只是一個「哈佛的事」，直到扎克伯格決定將其傳播到其他學校。扎克伯格和莫斯科維茨以及一些朋友搬到了加利福尼亞州帕洛阿爾托，他們租了一個小房子當辦公室。他們在 2004 年中期成立了第一個辦公室。於 2007，札克伯格 23 歲那年，他因為臉書的成功而成為億萬富翁。 臉書在 2012 年的全球用戶數量共達到一十億。

01
Part
飲食民生

02
Part
歷史懷舊

03
Part
現代實用科技

04
Part
資訊知識

必考字彙表

字彙	詞性	中譯	反義詞	中譯
Program	*v.*	電腦程式設計		
Hire	*v.*	雇用	Fire	解雇
Developer	*n.*	開發者		
Privately	*adv.*	私人地	Public	公開的
Graduate	*adj.*	研究所的		
Achieve	*v.*	完成	Fail	失敗
Reputation	*n.*	名聲		
Prodigy	*n.*	天才	Imbecile	弱智者
Sophomore	*n.*	大學二年級生		
Initially	*adv.*	開頭	Finally	最後
Launch	*v.*	開辦	Cease	停止
Drop out		退出	Carry on	繼續
Lease	*v.*	租賃		
Serve	*v.*	做為		

24-2 試題演練

牛刀小試

1. Parents try hard not to let their children get _____ to video games at their young age.

   B. close   B. addicting
   C. closely   D. addicted

2. I am going to walk around the conference and _____ with a few people.

   A. networking   B. socialize
   C. network   D. socialization

3. Sadly, her _____ has faded with time, and now she has been almost completely forgotten.

   A. famous   B. popular
   C. popularity   D. known

4. The rose in our garden is _____ and it smells wonderful.

   A. blossom   B. bloomed
   C. bloom   D. blooming

5. With her marvelous experiences, she was _____ for the job immediately.

   A. fired
   B. hired
   C. hiring
   D. got

6. When criticizing a friend, it should be done _____, but when praising one, it can be done publicly.

   A. public
   B. publicly
   C. private
   D. privately

7. He has a _____ as an excellent doctor so people are welling to wait in line for hours to see him.

   A. known
   B. name
   C. reputation
   D. saying

8. Companies often time _____ cars rather than buying them so that they could deduct the cost from tax.

   A. lease
   B. purchase
   C. rent
   D. rental

 **題目解析**

1. **(D)** 由句意可以理解應挑選有「沈溺」意味的字彙,而小孩是被動的」沈溺於,而不是主動的「使沈溺」,因此正確答案為 addicted。

2. **(C)** 由對等連接詞 and 得知此空格應填入動詞,因此應選擇 network,而不是 networking。

3. **(C)** 空格處應填入名詞,並由文句可知應填入「知名度」一詞,因此答案為 popularity。

4. **(D)** 空格處應填入 ving,因此答案為 blooming。

5. **(B)** 難句意為被動意思,但 a 選項 fired 不符合句意,由句意可以理解應選取有「錄取」意味的字彙。又由於是「被」錄取,因此應選取 hired 為解答。

6. **(D)** 此空格應填入副詞,因此 a 和 c 可以先行刪除,而由句意及字詞可以選出 privately 為正確解答。

7. **(C)** 由句意可以理解空格應填入「名聲」一詞,因此 reputation 為正確解答。

8. (A) 文中提及 could deduct the cost from tax 代替購買可減稅，因此答案不會為 purchase，應該為「租賃」。又因長期租賃在英語中慣用為 lease，所以答案為 a。

Unit 25 25-1
Telephone
電話
by *Alexander Graham Bell*

Telephone MP3 49

The paper cup telephone is a great childhood memory for most of us. Centuries ago, acoustic telephone, the earliest mechanical telephone was based on the same theory which utilized sound transmission through pipes. It connects two diaphragms with a string or wire and transmits sound by mechanical vibrations from one side to another.

Two hundred years later in 1876, Alexander Graham Bell was awarded him the first U.S. patent for the invention of the electrical telephone. Although the credit for the invention of the electric telephone is frequently disputed. Many other inventors such as Charles Bourseul, Antonio Meucci, and others have all been credited with the telephone invention.

By 1904 over three million phones were connected by manual switchboard exchanges in the United States. US became the world leader in telephone density. The telephone with bell and induction coil which we are familiar with was introduced in the 1930s. Another 30 years later, the touch-tone signaling replaced the rotary dial. In 1973, Motorola manager Martin Cooper placed the very first cellular phone call and began the era of the mobile phone. In 2008, over 290 million cell phones were sold worldwide. And after the first debut of smartphone, the boom just never seems to drop. When will the next generation telephone be invented? We are all excited to see.

電話

紙杯電話對我們大多數人來說是一個偉大的童年記憶。基於同樣的理論,聲覺電話幾百年前利用管線傳送聲音,是最早的機械電話。它是英國物理學家羅伯特・胡克於 1667 年利用細繩或金屬絲連接兩個隔膜,由機械振動的原理從一側傳送聲音到另一端。

200 年後的 1876 年,亞歷山大・格雷厄姆・貝爾獲得他第一個發明電話的專利。雖然這個電話發明的榮譽經常有爭議。許多其他的發明家,如查爾斯・布爾瑟,安東尼奧・穆齊,和其他人都被認為發明了電話。

到 1904 年,美國人工總機總共有超過三百萬個連結。美國的電話密度領先全球。我們所熟悉,有鈴聲和感應線圈的電話在 1930 年代引入。30 年後,按鍵信號取代旋轉撥號。 1973 年,摩托羅拉的經理馬丁・庫帕撥出第一通移動電話,開始了手機的時代。在 2008 年,全球的手機銷量超過 2.9 億。而智慧型手機第一次亮相後,手機的需求似乎永遠不會下降。下一代的電話又會在什麼時候被發明呢？我們都很期待。

必考字彙表

字彙	詞形	中譯	反義詞	中譯
Acoustic	*adj.*	原聲的		
Mechanical	*adj.*	機械驅動的	Manual	手動的
Transmission	*n.*	傳送		
Diaphragm	*n.*	隔膜		
Vibration	*n.*	震動	Stillness	靜止
Electrical	*adj.*	電的	Manual	手動的
Dispute	*n.*	爭論	Concord	和諧
Switchboard	*n.*	電話總機		
Density	*n.*	密度	Sparsity	稀疏
Signal	*v.*	發信號		
Rotary	*adj.*	旋轉的		
Cellular	*adj.*	蜂窩式的		
Debut	*n.*	首次亮相	Finale	終曲
Smartphone	*n.*	智慧型手機		

Alexander Graham Bell

MP3 50

Son of a phonetician, Alexander Graham Bell was born on March 3rd, 1847 in Edinburgh, Scotland. As many other inventors, Bell was a creative brilliant child who had shown curiosity about his world. His first invention was a dehusking machine which automatically dehusked wheat. He was only 12 at that time. At the same year, the hearing loss of Bell's mother led to his study in acoustics.

Bell moved to Canada in 1870 with his family. Three years later, Bell became a professor at Boston University specialized in voice physiology. Bell also taught deaf people how to speak, and because of that, he married Mabel Hubbard who was born deaf. Mabel Hubbard's father Gardiner Greene Hubbard was very wealthy. This gave Bell great help in his invention. In 1874, with his father-in-law and Thomas Sanders' financial support, Bell hired Thomas Watson as his assistant and started his research on Telephone. In 1876, Bell filed the patent for telephone. A year later, Bell, Hubbard, Sanders and Watson formed the Bell Telephone Company. Back then, people still couldn't see the practicality and outlook for telephone. Therefore, only hundreds of telephones were sold in the following years. Bell was not interested in doing business so he left the Bell Telephone company in 1879.

Bell passed away in 1922 at the age of 75. At that time, over 14 million telephones were installed in the United States. Undersea telephone and wireless telephones were

01
Part
飲食民生

02
Part
歷史懷舊

03
Part
現代實用科技

04
Part
資訊知識

also invented. Bell Telephone company became AT&T which is still the No.1 telephone company in the United States. In 1925, the president of AT&T, Walt JiFode acquired the research department of Western Electronics and set up a program called "Bell Telephone Laboratories." This lab contributed many new inventions with epochal meanings, such as transistors, solar cells LEDs, etc.

亞歷山大・格雷厄姆・貝爾

　　一個聲音學家的兒子，亞歷山大・格雷厄姆・貝爾於 1847 年 3 月 3 日出生於蘇格蘭的愛丁堡。正如許多其他的發明家，貝爾是一個聰明且具創意的孩子，並對他的世界表現出好奇。他的第一個發明是去麥殼機，可自動脫去小麥的殼。當時他只有 12 歲。同年，他的母親的聽覺喪失促使他研究聲音學。

　　貝爾在 1870 年時與他的家人一起移居加拿大。3 年後，貝爾成為了波士頓大學的教授專門從事語音生理學。貝爾還教聾人怎麼説話，正因為如此，他娶了天生就聽不到的梅布爾・哈伯德。梅布爾・哈伯德的父親加德納・格林・哈伯德是非常富裕的。這給了貝爾的發明很大的幫助。1874 年，由於他的岳父和托馬斯・桑德斯的資金支持，貝爾僱用了托馬斯・沃森作為他的助手，開始了他對電話的研究。1876 年，貝爾提出電話的專利。一年後，貝爾，哈伯德，桑德斯和沃森組成了貝爾電話公司。那時，人們還無法看到電話的實用性和前景。因此，只有幾百隻電話於次年銷售出去。貝爾對做生意沒有興趣，於是他於 1879 年離開了貝爾電話公司。

　　貝爾於 1992 年去世，享年 75 歲。當時已有 1400 多萬隻電話被安裝在美國。海底電話和無線電話也已發明了。貝爾電話公司後來成為ＡＴ＆Ｔ 公司，ＡＴ＆Ｔ 仍然是美國的第一大電話公司。1925 年，ＡＴ＆Ｔ 公司的總裁沃爾特收購了西方電子公司的研究部門，並成立了一個「貝爾電話實驗室。」這個實驗室貢獻了許多具有劃時代意義的新發明，例如晶體管、太陽能電池 LED 等。

 字彙

字彙	詞形	中譯	反義詞	中譯
Phonetician	*n.*	語音學家		
Dehusk	*v.*	去殼		
Specialize	*v.*	專攻	Broaden	延伸
Physiology	*n.*	生理學		
Wealthy	*adj.*	富有的	Poor	窮困的
Practicality	*n.*	實用性	Impracticality	不實用性
Outlook	*n.*	展望	Certainty	事實
Undersea	*adj.*	海底的		
Wireless	*adj.*	無線的	Landline	地上通訊線
Acquire	*v.*	獲得	Spend	花費
Contribute	*v.*	貢獻	Counteract	對抗
Epochal	*adj.*	劃時代的	Regular	一般的

01
Part
飲食民生

02
Part
歷史懷舊

03
Part
現代實用科技

04
Part
資訊知識

25-2　試題演練

牛刀小試

1. Touchscreen replaces the _____ lever in many machines.

    A. manual　　　　　B. human

    C. mechanical　　　D. machine

2. The _____ of diseases might be invisible.

    A. transmit　　　　B. transition

    C. transfer　　　　D. transmission

3. Taiwan and Japan have been _____ for years over an island.

    A. fought　　　　　B. disputing

    C. fighting　　　　D. disputed

4. One half of the earth has a greater _____ than the other.

    A. population　　　B. density

    C. people　　　　　D. resource

5. Most glass cutting machines contain _____ movements of the blades.

   A. round   B. rotary

   C. rotaries   D. revolve

6. _____ is often more important than theory.

   A. Practicality   B. Practice

   C. Practical   D. Theoretical

7. Any guns that _____ by gift or by will have to be registered.

   A. given   B. acquired

   C. purchased   D. bought

8. Television is an _____ invention.

   A. standard   B. establish

   C. epochal   D. history

01
Part
飲食民生

02
Part
歷史懷舊

03
Part
現代實用科技

04
Part
資訊知識

題目解析

1. (C) 空白處應填入形容詞並為觸控式的相反詞,因此 mechanical 為正確答案,A選項manual B選項human, D選項machine 均不符合文意。

2. (D) a 和 c 均為動詞故不選,比較 b 和 d 後,由文句翻譯可知空白處應填入「傳染」一詞的名詞,因此解答為 transmission。表示疾病的傳遞是肉眼所不可見的。

3. (B) 空白處應填入主動的 v + ing,而「dispute」一字會比「fight」適當,因此 disputing 為正確答案,A 選項 fought,C 選項 fighting,D 選項 disputed 均不符合。

4. (B) 此文要說明的是人口的集中度,因此解答為 density,A 選項 population,C 選項 people,D 選項 resource 均不符合。

5. (B) 句意須填入形容詞故空格應填入形容 movements 的形容詞,因此 rotary 最為適當。

6. (A) 空格是主詞,因此應填入名詞,故 c 和 d 均為 adj 故不考慮,所以答案為 a 或 b。由文句及字彙則可判斷出 practicality 是正確解答。

7. (B) 此處應該填入「獲得」一詞,因此解答為 acquired,A 選項 given,C 選項 purchsed,D 選項 bought 均不符合文意。

8. (C) 空白處應為形容 invention 的形容詞，電視又為一個偉大的發明，所以 epochal 較為適當的選項，A 選項 standard，B 選項 establish，D 選項 history 均不符合。

01
Part
飲食民生

02
Part
歷史懷舊

03
Part
現代實用科技

04
Part
資訊知識

Unit 26 26-1
Online Banking
線上銀行
by Stanford Federal Credit Union

Online Banking

MP3 51

In today's highly technical world, banks are no longer a brick-and-mortar financial institution. From remittance to investment, people nowadays only need to go thru online banking to finish all these works. The concept of online banking has been simultaneously evolving with the development of the World Wide Web, and has actually been accessible around since the early 1980s.

In 1981, the four biggest banks in New York City Citibank, Chase Manhattan, Chemical and Manufacturers Hanover, made the home banking access available to their customers. However, customers didn't really take to the initiative. The innovative way of doing business was too advanced and failed to gain momentum until the mid 1990s. In October, 1994, Stanford Federal Credit Union offered online banking to all its customers, and about a year later, Presidential Bank offered their customers online account accesses. These were the start of online banking, and soon other banks followed.

Though customers were hesitant to use online banking at first. Most of the people didn't trust its security feature. Up until today, some people still have the same concern. It was after the e-commerce started to popularize did the idea of online banking slowly began to catch on. By the year of 2000, an overwhelmingly 80% of banks in the U.S. offered online banking services. In 2001, Bank of America gained more than 3 million online banking customers, about 20% of its customer base. Online banking effectively decreases overhead costs to offer more competitive rates and enjoys higher profit margins. It now becomes so widespread all over the world and allows many investors to operate their assets around the world with no time difference issues.

網路銀行

在當今高科技的世界裡，銀行不再是實體的金融機構。從匯款到投資，人們現在只需要上網路銀行就可以完成所有的工作。網路銀行這一概念與全球資訊網一同發展演變，自 1980 年代初期就已經出現。

在 1981 年，紐約的四大銀行，花旗銀行、大通曼哈頓銀行、化工銀行和製造漢諾威銀行提供了家庭銀行給他們的客戶。但客戶並沒有真正採取行動。這個生意方式的創新太過先進，直到 1990 年代中期都沒能獲得新的動力。1994 年 10 月，史丹佛的聯邦信貸聯盟提供了所有的客戶網上銀行，大約一年後，總統銀行提供客戶網銀的服務。這就是網路銀行的開始。不久後其他銀行隨即跟進。

不過，顧客們一開始並不願意使用網路銀行。大多數人並不相信它的安全功能。直到今天，有些人仍然有同樣的擔憂。這是自從電子商務開始流行後，網路銀行的想法才開始慢慢流行起來。直到 2000 年，在美國有壓倒性有 80%的銀行都提供網路銀行的服務。在 2001 年，美國銀行擁有了 300 多萬網路銀行客戶。這是約 20%的客戶群。網上銀行有效地降低管理成本，提供更具競爭力的價格，並享受更高的利潤。它現在在世界各地已經非常普及也讓許多投資者可以避免時差問題，在世界各地運營資產。

必考字彙表

字彙	詞形	中譯	反義詞	中譯
Brick-and-mortar	*adj.*	實體的	Fictitious	虛擬的
Remittance	*n.*	匯款		
Investment	*n.*	投資	Divestment	脫去
Simultaneously	*adv.*	同時地	Separately	分開地
Access	*n.*	入口	Outlet	出口
Initiative	*adj.*	創始的		
Advanced	*adj.*	先進的	Traditional	傳統的
Momentum	*n.*	動力	Brake	制動
Hesitant	*adj.*	猶豫的	Decisive	決定性的
Security	*n.*	保障		
e-commerce	*n.*	電子商務		

Popularize	v.	使普及		
Overwhelming	adj.	無法抗拒的	Insignificant	無足輕重的
Overhead	adj.	管理的		
Margin	n.	利潤		
Widespread	adj.	廣泛的	Limited	有限的
Asset	n.	資產		

01
Part
飲食民生

02
Part
歷史懷舊

03
Part
現代實用科技

04
Part
資訊知識

Stanford Federal Credit Union

MP3 52

Stanford Federal Credit Union is a federally chartered credit union located in Palo Alto, California which provides banking services to the Stanford community. Stanford Federal Credit Union was created by a group of Stanford University employees. On Dec 1959, the credit union only opened to the university employees in 1960 with $261 in deposits. In both 1985 and 2004, it respectively expanded its field of membership to student and employee members and members of library, but was still not yet opened to the public.

Even though, the credit union is relatively small, it is famous for its advance services over years. In the late 1970s, Stanford Federal Credit Union offered one of the first checking accounts and credit cards. In the early 1980s, it introduced ATMs and banking by telephone. In November

1993, it conducted its first four internet transactions; and in 1994, it became the first financial institution to offer online banking when it launched its website. Three years later, it offered online BillPay to its members, and in 2002, it added account aggregation and mobile banking. The amazing works didn't stop there. It 2005, it became one of the first institutions to implement the Passmark authentication system, and 2 years later, it joined the CO-OP network to provide its members with over 30,000 surcharge-free ATMs worldwide.

Located at the Silicon Valley and gathered the most intelligent engineers, Stanford Federal Credit Union always arouses the most innovative banking systems. We look forward to the next crazy idea it might come up with.

史丹佛聯邦信用合作社

史丹佛聯邦信用合作社是一家位於加州帕洛阿爾托，給史丹佛社區提供金融服務的聯邦特許儲蓄合作社。由史丹佛員工所創立，1960年，信用合作社只開放給大學雇員，開戶需存 261 美元。

雖然，信用合作社的規模相對比較小，它多年來的先進服務卻很出名。在 1970 年代尾，史丹佛聯邦信用合作社提供了第一個支票賬戶和第一張信用卡之一。在 1980 年代初期，它推出了自動提款機和電話銀行。1993 年 11 月，它進行了前四個網上交易，並於 1994 年，成為第一個提供網上銀行的金融機構。3 年後，它提供了他的成員網上的 **BillPay**，並在 2002 年，增加了帳戶的聚集和移動銀行。令人驚奇的作品並沒有就此停止。它在 2005 年成為 **Passmark** 認證系統中的第一機構之一。2 年後，它加入了 **CO-OP** 網絡，為會員提供全球超過 30,000 座免費自動提款機。

位於矽谷並聚集了最聰明的工程師，史丹佛聯邦信用合作社始終能激發出最具創新性的銀行體系。我們期待著它可能會想出的下一個瘋狂想法。

字彙

字彙	詞形	中譯	反義詞	中譯
Chartered	*adj.*	領有執照的		
Community	*n.*	社區		
Deposit	*v.*	存款	Withdraw	提款
Expand	*v.*	擴大	Compress	壓縮
Relatively	*adv.*	相對地		
Conduct	*v.*	引導	Mismanagement	管理不當
Transaction	*n.*	交易		
Aggregation	*n.*	集成體		
Implement	*n.*	實施	Cancel	取消
Authentication	*n.*	證實		

26-2 試題演練

1. Many twins are _____ and characteristically similar.

   A. physical   B. look
   C. physically   D. outside

2. Facebook no longer allowed people to register with _____ names.

   A. brick-and-mortar B. realistic
   C. fictitious   D. pretend

3. In March of 1986, more than 6,000 radio stations in the U.S played the song "We are the World" _____ to raise money to help with an African famine relief project.

   A. gradually   B. simultaneously
   C. simply   D. gently

4. His mother's appearance gave him _____ to continue on the race.

   A. discourage   B. encourage
   C. momentum   D. action

5. Please do not _____ to contact me if you need any help.

   A. Hesitant   B. Hesitation
   C. Hesitate   D. Hesitated

6. The company was _____ by more than 1,000 applicants for 10 positions.

   A. surprise   B. overwhelmed
   C. surprising   D. overwhelming

7. Heat is _____ more quickly by water than by air.

   A. conducting   B. transferring
   C. conducted   D. transferred

8. The new government has _____ a number of cutbacks to the military budget.

   A. discontinued   B. engaged
   C. reconsider   D. implemented

1. (A) 以對等連接詞連接應該是連接兩個副詞，空格應和 characteristically 相對應的副詞，因此解答為 physically，A 選項 physical，B 選項 look，D 選項 outside 均不符合文意。

2. (C) 空格應填入形容詞，而 d 為動詞故可刪，空格應填入「虛擬的」一詞，因此 fictitious 為正確答案。表示臉書不再允許人們以虛構的名字註冊。

3. (B) 由句意及字彙可得知 simultaneously 為正確答案，A 選項 gradually，C 選項 simply，D 選項 gently 均不符合文意。

4. (C) 空格應填入名詞，而由句意及字彙可得知 momentum 為正確解答。表示他母親的容貌給了他繼續比賽的動力，A 選項 discourage，C 選項 encourage，D 選項 action 均不符合文意。

5. (C) 空格應填入動詞原型，因此答案為 hesitate。表示若需要任何幫助，別猶豫與我聯繫。

6. (B) 空格應為被動，句型為 S＋V＋p.p…因此答案為 overwhelmed，A 選項 surprise，C 選項 surprising，D 選項 overwhelming 均不符合文意。

7. (C) 由句意可知 conduct 為正確的字彙，由文法則可得知 conducted 為正確選項。表是熱能在空氣中傳導的速度快於水，A 選項 conducting，B 選項 transferring，D 選項 transferred 均不符合文意。

8. (D) 句型為 S＋has＋p.p⋯，而 c 選項為動詞故可刪，而由句意可知 implemented 為最合適的選項。

01
Part
飲食民生

02
Part
歷史懷舊

03
Part
現代實用科技

04
Part
資訊知識

Unit 27 27-1
Printing Press
印刷機
by *Johannes Gutenberg*

Printing Press MP3 53

Without the invention of the printing press, we would have very limited amount of books, newspapers, or magazines, and information and knowledge would be hard to expand to society.

Printing technology was developed during the 1300s to 1400s. People cut letter or images on blocks of wood, dipped in ink and then stamped onto paper. Around 1440, Inventor Johannes Gutenberg had the thought of using cut blocks within a machine to make the printing process faster. Since he worked at a mint before, he created metal blocks instead of wood, and was able to move the metal blocks to create new words and sentences with the movable type machine. Therefore, the first printed book was created – the Gutenberg Bible. The mechanization of bookmaking led to the first mass production of books in Europe. It could produce 3,600 pages per day which is much more productive than the typographic block type.

The demand of printing presses kept expanding through

out Europe. By 1500, more than twenty million volumes were produced. And the number kept doubling every year. The operation of a printing press became synonymous with the enterprise of printing and lent its name to a new branch of media, the press. In the 19th century, steam-powered rotary presses replaced the hand operated presses. It allowed high volume industrial scale printing.

Because of the invention of printing press, the entire classical canon was reprinted and promulgated throughout Europe. It was a very important step towards the democratization of knowledge. Also because of the invention of printing press, it helped unified and standardize the spelling and syntax of vernaculars.

印刷機

　　若沒有印刷機的發明，我們所能擁有的書、報紙或雜誌將會非常有限，而且訊息和知識很難於社會上傳播。

　　印刷技術是在 1300 年代到 1400 年代間被發明出來的。人們在木頭塊上刻印字母或圖像，沾墨，然後印在紙上。大約在 1440 年左右，發明家約翰・古騰堡有了將切割塊放在機器中，使打印過程加快的想法。由於他之前在造幣廠工作過，於是他利用金屬塊代替木材，並利用移動式的機器，使金屬塊可以移動，創造出單字或句子。因此，第一本

01
Part
飲食民生

02
Part
歷史懷舊

03
Part
現代實用科技

04
Part
資訊知識

印刷書籍古騰堡聖經就這樣被創造出來。造書的機械化帶領了歐洲書籍的大規模生產。它可以每天生產 3,600 頁，它比印刷塊的類型有更高的生產力。

印刷機的需求在整個歐洲不斷增加。到 1500 年代，超過兩千萬本書被製作出來。而數字每年保持翻倍成長。印刷機更與印刷企業劃上等號，因此新媒體的分支－新聞界－也分用同一個名詞「The Press」。在 19 世紀時，蒸汽動力輪轉印刷機取代了手工操作的印刷機。它實現了大批量的工業規模印刷。

由於印刷術的發明，整個古典經文已被重印並廣傳整個歐洲。這也是對知識民主化來說非常重要的一步。印刷術發明的同時，它也幫助統一和規範俗語的拼寫和語法。

必考字彙表

字彙	詞形	中譯	反義詞	中譯
Expend	*v.*	散播	Accumulate	累績
Mint	*n.*	造幣廠		
Movable	*v.*	可移動式的	Immovable	固定的
Mechanization	*n.*	機械化		
Productive	*adj.*	生產的	Destructive	破壞的
Typographic	*adj.*	排字的		
Synonymous	*adj.*	同義的	Different	不同的
Enterprise	*n.*	事業		
Branch	*n.*	分支	Headquarters	總部

Press	*n.*	新聞界		
Canon	*n.*	教規		
Promulgate	*v.*	廣傳	Suppress	隱瞞
Democratization	*n.*	民主化		
Unify	*v.*	統一	Divide	劃分
Syntax	*n.*	語法		
Vernacular	*n.*	俗語		

01
Part
飲食民生

02
Part
歷史懷舊

03
Part
現代實用科技

04
Part
資訊知識

Johannes Gutenberg MP3 54

Johannes Gutenberg was born in an upper-class family in Mainz Germany, most likely in 1398. He had been a blacksmith, a goldsmith, and printer, and even a publisher. Gutenberg's understanding about the trade of goldsmithing and possessing of the knowledge and technical skills in metal working originated from his father's working at ecclesiastic mint.

In 1411, there was an uprising in Mainz against the patricians. Unfortunately, Gutenberg was one of the family that was forced to leave. As a result, Gutenberg might have moved to Eltiville am Rhein, where his mother had an inherited estate there. Evidence had shown that he was instructing a wealthy tradesman on polishing gems in 1437. A couple of years later, he started his career in making polished metal mirrors. It was the same year that Gutenberg made the first movable printing press and introduce this technology to Europe.

His epochal inventions including movable printing press, oil-based ink for book printing, adjustable molds, etc., allowed the economical mass production of printed books. Gutenberg's printing technology spread rapidly throughout Europe and later the world. Gutenberg died in 1468 and was buried in his hometown Mainz. Unfortunately, the church he was buried got destroyed and his grave is now lost.

約翰・古騰堡

　　約翰・古騰堡出生於德國美因茨的一個上流家庭。他當過鐵匠、金匠和印刷商，甚至出版商。因為他的父親在傳教士的造幣廠工作過，因此古騰堡在長大過程中就了解金匠的行業，並擁有金屬加工的知識和技術技能。

　　1411 年，美因茨發動了對貴族的起義。不幸的，古騰堡就是其中一個被迫離開的家庭。因此，古騰堡可能已經搬離到萊茵河畔的艾莉菲爾，在那裡有他的母親所繼承的遺產。有證據表明，在 1437 年，他正在指導一個富商拋光寶石的技能。幾年後，他表示他以做拋光金屬鏡子為職業。同一年，古騰堡開發出第一個活動印刷機並將這種技術引入歐洲。

　　他劃時代的發明，包括活動印刷機、印刷書所用的油性油墨、可調節模具等，皆使印刷書籍能大批量的經濟生產。古騰堡印刷技術在整個歐洲及爾後的世界迅速蔓延。古騰堡在 1468 去世，並被安葬在他的家鄉美因茨。不幸的是，他下葬的教堂被破壞，他的墳墓現在已經消失。

必考字彙表

字彙	詞性	中譯	反義詞	中譯
Upper-class	*ph.*	上流社會	Lower-class	下層社會
Blacksmith	*n.*	鐵匠		
Goldsmith	*n.*	金匠		
Ecclesiastic	*n.*	傳教士		
Upraise	*v.*	上升	Deaden	削弱
Patrician	*n.*	貴族	Commoner	平民
Inherit	*v.*	繼承	Bequeath	遺留下
Estate	*n.*	地產		
Evidence	*n.*	證據	Concealment	隱瞞
Instruct	*v.*	命令		
Epochal	*adj.*	劃時代的	Constant	不變的
Adjustable	*adj.*	可調整的	Fixed	固定的
Destroy	*v.*	損壞	Build	建造

01
Part
飲食民生

02
Part
歷史懷舊

03
Part
現代實用科技

04
Part
資訊知識

27-2 試題演練

牛刀小試

1. Sales people always _____ a lot of air-miles during business trips and use them for personal trips.

   A. gather   B. collect
   C. accumulate   D. expend

2. Toys with _____ arms and legs are popular with kids.

   A. stiff   B. firm
   C. conceal   D. movable

3. Since we were kids, we were taught that wealth is not necessarily _____ with happiness.

   A. different   B. synonymous
   C. syncretic   D. separate

4. Entrepreneurs normally don't _____ their political beliefs.

   A. public   B. hide
   C. cover up   D. promulgate

5. No one can foresee when North Korea will start the country's _____.

A. communism   B. democratization
C. communist   D. democratic

6. He lost all his _____ gambling on the stock market.

A. inherit   B. inherited
C. inheritance   D. inheritances

7. The law requires enough _____ to charge a person.

A. truth   B. evidence
C. story   D. episode

8. His confidence was completely _____ after falling the test.

A. destruction   B. destroy
C. destructive   D. destroyed

01 Part 飲食民生

02 Part 歷史懷舊

03 Part 現代實用科技

04 Part 資訊知識

題目解析

1. (C) 由句意可知空白處應填入「收集」一詞，須注意 a, b, c 均為收集，但當使用於里程數的收集時應用 accumulate 一詞，A 選項 gather，B 選項 collect，D 選項 expend 均不符合文意。

2. (D) c 選項為動詞故不考慮，四個形容詞中唯一一個表示「可動的」字為 moveable，因此為正確解答，A 選項 stiff B 選項 firm，C 選項 conceal 均不符合文意。

3. (B) 空白處應填入形容詞，並由句意我們可以選出 synonymous 為正確答案。Be synonymous with 為…與…一致，為常考用法，A 選項 different，C 選項 syncretic，D 選項 separate 均不符合文意。

4. (A) 4 個選項均為動詞，文句中的 Don't 點出 Entrepreneurs 不希望之處，因此答案為 public。表示公開他們的政治理念，B 選項 public，C 選項 cover up，D 選項 promulgate 均不符合文意。

5. (B) Country's 後應接名詞，而 No one can foresee 又說明北韓不可遇見的將來，因此解答為 democratization，A 選項 given，C 選項 purchsed，D 選項 bought 均不符合文意。

6. (C) his 為所有格其後加名詞故空白處應填入名詞，因此正確答案
為 c 或 d，又因 inheritance 不可數，因此 c 為正確答案。

7. (B) 由句意得知空白應填入 evidence 最為適合，A選項truth，C
選項 story，D 選項 destroyed 均不符合文意。

8. (D) 空白應填入被動詞，句構為 S＋bev＋adv＋p.p，因此
destroyed 為正確答案。

01
Part
飲食民生

02
Part
歷史懷舊

03
Part
現代實用科技

04
Part
資訊知識

Unit 28 28-1
Television
電視
by *Philo Taylor Farnsworth*

Television   MP3 55

From the number of TV audiences in each American household, televisions not only provide entertainments and all kinds of information, but also have become a daily necessity.

The word television comes from the Greek prefix "tele" and the Latin word "vision". It converts images into electrical impulses along cables, or by radio waves or satellite to a receiver, and then they are changed back into picture. As most inventions, more than one individuals contributed to the development of television. The earliest development was recorded in the late 1800s. A German student, Paul Gottlieb Nipkow, developed the first mechanical module of television. He sent images through wires with the help of a rotating metal disk. It only had 18 lines of resolution. In 1926, a Scottish amateur scientist, John Logie Baird, transmitted the first moving pictures through the mechanical disk system. In 1934, all television systems had converted into the electronic system, which is what is being used even today. An American inventor, Philo Taylor Farnsworth first

01
Part
飲食民生

02
Part
歷史懷舊

03
Part
現代實用科技

04
Part
資訊知識

had the idea of electronic television at the age of 14. By the time he was 21, he created the first electronic television system which is the basis of all TV we have today. Until the 1900s, all TVs were monochrome. In 1925, color television was just conceptualized, but never been built. It was not until 1953 did color television become available to the public.

In the late 1990s, the bulky, high-voltage CRT screen was replaced by energy efficient, flat-panel screens, such as plasma screens, LCDs, and OLEDs. In the mid-2010s, major manufacturers announced to discontinue the CRT TVs. Now manufactures again brain stormed and built in the smart TV system so televisions now not only provide TV problems but also can be used as computer. What will come next? We shall wait and see.

💡 電視

　從每個美國家庭電視收看觀眾的數量來看，電視不只提供娛樂和各種訊息，而且成了每日必需品。

　電視這個字源自於希臘語字首的「遠程」和拉丁字「願景」的組合。它將圖像轉換成電脈衝沿著電纜，或通過無線電波或衛星到接收器，然後將它們再變回為圖像。如同大部分的發明，許多人都對電視的發展有所貢獻。最早的發展記錄是在 19 世紀末期。一位德國學生，保羅・戈特利布・尼普可夫研製了第一台電視的機械模塊。他透過電線與旋轉金屬盤發送圖像。它只有 18 線的分辨率。 1926 年，蘇格蘭業餘科學家，約翰・勞基・貝瑞德透過機械磁盤系統發送出第一個動畫。1934 年，所有的電視系統已轉換成電子系統，這即是今天被使用的系統。美國發明家，菲洛・泰勒・法恩斯沃思在 14 歲時便有了電子電視的想法。在 21 歲時，他創造了第一個電子電視系統，這是所有我們今天所擁有的所有電視的基礎。直到 1900 年代，所有的電視都還是黑白的。 1925 年時彩色電視都還只是概念，從來沒有被製造過。直到 1953 年，彩色電視才被提供給一般消費者。

在 1990 年代後期，高效節能的平板螢幕，如離子顯示器、液晶顯示器，和 OLED 被發明出來。這種進化發展取代了笨重、高電壓的 CRT 電視。在 2010 年代中期，各大廠商宣布停止 CRT 電視的製造。現在電視生產大廠再次的發想，並建立了智能電視系統，電視不只提供電視而已，而且還可以作為電腦。接下來會有什麼樣的發展呢？我們拭目以待。

必考字彙表

字彙	詞形	中譯	反義詞	中譯
Necessity	*n.*	必要性	Auxiliary	輔助的
Entertainment	*n.*	娛樂	Boredom	無聊
Prefix	*n.*	字首		
Convert	*v.*	轉換		
Impulse	*n.*	脈衝		

Satellite	*n.*	衛星		
Receiver	*n.*	接收器	Transmitter	發射器
Individual	*adj.*	個人的	Collective	聚集而成的
Contribute	*v.*	貢獻	Counteract	對抗
Resolution	*n.*	解析度		
Amateur	*adj.*	業餘的	Professional	專業的
Transmit	*v.*	傳送	Receive	接收
Monochrome	*n.*	黑白	Color	彩色
Conceptualize	*adj.*	概念的		

Philo Taylor Farnsworth

MP3 56

A talented inventor that came up with the television system idea at the age of 14, Philo Taylor Farnsworth was born on August 19th, 1906, in Beaver, Utah. When he was in high school, he won a national contest with his original invention of a tamper-proof lock. He sketched out the television idea from a vacuum tube in his chemistry class during high school but none of his teachers grasped the implications of his concept.

Farnsworth then entered the Brigham Young University in 1922 but due to his father's death, he dropped out 2 years later. In 1926, he moved to San Francisco to continue his scientific work, and a year later, he unveiled his electronic television prototype made by a "Image dissector", which he had sketched in his chemistry class in high school.

Throughout the late 1920s and the early 1930s, Farnsworth fought legal charges that his inventions were in violation of a patent by the inventor Vloadimir Zoworkyin a patent that was later on owned by RCA. Farnsworth later on moved to Philadelphia for a position at Philco and left Philco company in 1933 to pursue his own avenues of research. He eventually won the lawsuit and received a million dollars from RCA. He ran a fusion lab at Utah 29 years later and operated under the name of Philo T. Farnsworth Association in Salty Lake City the following year. Unfortunately, he suffered from depression and became an alcoholic in his late years due to his serious debt.

菲洛・泰勒・法恩斯沃斯

　　一個才華橫溢的發明家，在 14 歲時便有了電視系統的想法，菲洛・泰勒・法恩斯沃斯在 1906 年 8 月 19 號出生於猶他州的比佛。當他在高中時，他防篡改鎖的發明使他贏得了全國比賽。他從化學課的真空管中勾勒出電視的想法，但沒有一位老師抓到他概念的含義。

　　法恩斯沃思隨後在 1922 年進入楊百翰大學，但由於他父親的過世，他 2 年後放棄了學業。1926 年，他移居舊金山，繼續他的科學工作，而一年之後，他利用他在高中時所勾勒出的「析像儀」，他推出了自己的電子電視。

在 1920 年末期和 1930 年代初期，法恩斯沃思被指控侵犯發明人 Vloadimir Zoworkyin 的專利，這個專利後來由 RCA 所擁有。法恩斯沃思後來在 1933 年實為了追求自己的研究，離開了菲戈公司。他最終贏得了官司，並從 RCA 獲得一百萬美元。二十九年後他於猶他州管理一個融合實驗室且於次年以裴洛 T. 法恩斯沃斯協會之名在鹽城湖運作。不幸地是，他晚年因龐大的債務而受憂鬱症的折磨，並成了酒鬼。

字彙

字彙	詞形	中譯	反義詞	中譯
Tamper	*v.*	竄改	Remain	維持
Sketch	*n.*	草稿		
Grasp	*v.*	理解	Misconception	誤解
Implication	*n.*	含義		
Unveil	*v.*	揭露	Conceal	隱蔽
Throughout	*Prep.*	遍佈		
Violation	*n.*	侵犯	Obedience	服從
Pursue	*v.*	追求	Give up	放棄
Avenue	*n.*	途徑		
Fusion	*n.*	融合	Separation	分裂
Operate	*v.*	營業		
Depression	*n.*	憂鬱症	Happiness	歡樂
Alcoholic	*n.*	酒鬼		

01
Part
飲食民生

02
Part
歷史懷舊

03
Part
現代實用科技

04
Part
資訊知識

28-2 試題演練

 牛刀小試

1. A decent family is a basic _____ in life.

   A. luxury   B. necessity
   C. Auxiliary   D. Request

2. The _____ industry seems glamorous and exciting on the outside, but in reality it is hard work.

   A. television   B. entertainment
   C. show   D. performance

3. Most of the international flights now have _____ entertainment systems which make flying more pleasant.

   A. group   B. person
   C. individual   D. children

4. The young politician is having a hard time responding to the press because he is an _____ at manipulating public opinion.

   A. expert   B. student
   C. amateur   D. instructor

5. After studied 4 years of computer engineering, he had a good _____ of computer programming.

   A. understood   B. grasp

   C. interest   D. ability

6. The government has _____ plans for new education program for teenagers.

   A. veiled   B. concealed

   C. unveiled   D. veil

7. The whole world was worried that the computer system would not _____ when crossing the Millennium.

   A. operate   B. crash

   C. break down   D. turn on

8. Carol has been an _____ for over 10 years. She finally checked into the rehab facility and hopefully can quite the habit for good.

   A. vegan   B. macrobiotic

   C. alcoholic   D. fruitarian

01 Part 飲食民生

02 Part 歷史懷舊

03 Part 現代實用科技

04 Part 資訊知識

題目解析

1. (B) 由句意可得知空格應填入「需求」的名詞，因此正確答案為 necessity，A 選項 luxury，C 選項 auxiliary，D 選項 request 均不符合文意。

2. (B) 這裡所要闡述的為「娛樂圈」，因此 entertainment 為正確答案。表示娛樂圈在外在似乎很光鮮亮麗且令人感到興奮，但現實中它卻是苦力，A 選項 television，C 選項 show，D 選項 performance 均不符合文意。

3. (C) 空格應填入形容詞，因此解答為 individual 表示大部分的國際航班現在有娛樂系統使得飛行更為舒適。

4. (C) 句首的 young politician 説明了他是經驗不足的，因此解答為 amateur。

5. (B) 由句意及字彙可以簡單找出 grasp 為正確答案，表示對…有好的掌握，A 選項 lunderstood，C 選項 interest，D 選項 ability 均不符合文意，另一個常見的用法有 with good command of English。

6. (C) has 之後應該接 v+ed，因此選擇應為 a，b 或 c。由句意可以了解政府是「發表了」新的政策，因此 unveiled 為正解，A 選項 veiled，B 選項 concealed，D 選項 veil 均不符合文意。

7. (A) 由句意及字彙即可簡單得知 operate 為正確解答。表示整個世界都擔心著電腦系統在跨越千禧年時會無法運作，B 選項 crash，C 選項 break down，D 選項 turn on 均不符合文意。

8. (C) 在第二句的 check in to rehab 清楚地說明答案為 alcoholic，A 選項 vegan，B 選項 macrobiotic，D 選項 fruitarian 均不符合文意。

01
Part
飲食民生

02
Part
歷史懷舊

03
Part
現代實用科技

04
Part
資訊知識

Leader 045

影響力字彙 (MP3)

作　　者	洪婉婷
發 行 人	周瑞德
執行總監	齊心瑀
企劃編輯	陳韋佑
校　　對	編輯部
封面構成	高鍾琪

內頁構成	菩薩蠻數位文化有限公司
印　　製	大亞彩色印刷製版股份有限公司
初　　版	2016 年 6 月
定　　價	新台幣 380 元
出　　版	力得文化
電　　話	(02) 2351-2007
傳　　真	(02) 2351-0887
地　　址	100 台北市中正區福州街 1 號 10 樓之 2
E - m a i l	best.books.service@gmail.com
網　　址	www.bestbookstw.com

港澳地區總經銷	泛華發行代理有限公司
地　　　　址	香港新界將軍澳工業邨駿昌街 7 號 2 樓
電　　　　話	(852) 2798-2323
傳　　　　真	(852) 2796-5471

國家圖書館出版品預行編目資料

影響力字彙 / 洪婉婷著. -- 初版. -
臺北市：力得文化, 2016.06
面　　；　　公　分 . --
(Leader ; 45)
ISBN 978-986-92856-4-3 (平
裝附光碟片)
1. 英語 2. 詞彙
　805.12　　　　　　　105008087